The Dream-

ALSO BY KIJ JOHNSON

The Fox Woman
Fudoki
Dragon's Honor (with Greg Cox)

COLLECTIONS
At the Mouth of the River of Bees

THE
DREAM-QUEST
OF
VELLITT BOE

KIJ JOHNSON

A TOM DOHERTY ASSOCIATES BOOK

NEW YORK

This is a work of fiction. All of the characters, organizations, and events portrayed in this novella are either products of the author's imagination or are used fictitiously.

THE DREAM-QUEST OF VELLITT BOE

Copyright © 2016 by Kij Johnson

Cover art by Victo Ngai
Cover design by Christine Foltzer

Map by Serena Malyon

Edited by Jonathan Strahan

A Tor.com Book
Published by Tom Doherty Associates, LLC
175 Fifth Avenue
New York, NY 10010

www.tor.com

Tor® is a registered trademark of Tom Doherty Associate, LLC.

ISBN 978-0-7653-8651-9 (ebook)
ISBN 978-0-7653-9141-4 (trade paperback)

First Edition: August 2016

For everyone who had to find her own way in

The Dream-Quest of Vellitt Boe

VELLITT BOE WAS DREAMING of a highway and ten million birds in an empty sky of featureless blue. The highway, broad and black as a tar pit. The birds, a cloud of them, like a mist writhing, like gnats pillaring over the dark marshes of Lomar or flickering shoals of silver fish in the crystal seas beyond Oriab. The sky: empty, untextured, flat. A great black beast crouching beside her growled steadily, but the birds were louder. One called with a high sweet voice, and it was saying, "Professor Boe? Professor Boe!"

Reality returned in rapid stages: the never-absent pain in her back; the softness against her face of sheets worn satin-smooth in the College's laundry; the cold air; the moonlight graphed by the casemented windows onto the broad bare floor of her dark bedroom; the percussion of urgent fists; and the voice, soprano but strong—one of the students and afraid, so afraid: "Professor! Please, O gods, please, you *must* wake up!"

And she was awake. Vellitt pushed herself upright in her narrow bed. "Wait!" she called, caught her robe from where it lay across her feet, and stepped into her slippers.

Kij Johnson

She went to open the door.

It was Derysk Oure, the third-year Chymical Studies scholar, one hand still raised from the knocking. In the sallow light of the hallway's single gas-jet, her face was the color of drying mud, and more anxious than Vellitt had ever seen it. She was dressed in a pyjama suit—quite daring, really—but with a country shawl around her shoulders, and she was weeping. "Professor Boe! Please, please come right away! I don't— It's Jurat."

Food-poisoning in the Hall, scandal, suicide: there were a thousand ways a women's college might find itself destroyed. Clarie Jurat was a third-year, reading Mathematics with Vellitt, and her best student in twenty years of teaching at Ulthar Women's College: a brilliant girl, strong-willed, charismatic and beautiful, with long laughing eyes and thick black hair she wore always in a heavy fishtail braid half down her back.

"Lead me." Vellitt followed Oure down the stairwell, the girl still sobbing. "What about Jurat? Calm *down*, Oure, or I'll have you on my hands, as well. This is not the way an Ulthar woman behaves."

Oure paused, pressed her palms against her eyes. "I know, I'm sorry, Professor. You're right. I was on my way to bed, and Hust burst out of their suite just as I was going past, and she said, *She's gone, she's run away with him,* so Martveit ran to get the Dean, and I came to get you. I

14

don't know anything else."

"Jurat takes Exams in three months. When did she have *time* to meet anyone?"

Oure turned back down the stairs. "I don't know, I'm sure." It was a lie, of course, but the girl said no more.

They exited Fellow's Stair and crossed the quad. Only one set of lights shone out, from Jurat's windows. Good; the fewer awake in the first uncontrolled moments of this situation—whatever it was—the better. The shadows were all moving, visibly shifting as the moon drifted southward on some god's whim. The cold night air was filled with the sharp scents of chrysanthemums and the first fallen leaves, and was so quiet that Vellitt could hear cats wailing just beyond the College wall. A clowder had congregated within the quad, as well; they ceased whatever was their business and watched as Vellitt and Oure passed, and one, a small black cat, separated itself from the rest and followed them into Jurat's stairwell. The cold light streaming in through the windows vanished suddenly as the moon passed behind the dining-hall's tower, and they were left in the flickering amber of the weak gas-jets on each landing.

A handful of young women had clustered near Jurat's door, wrapped in bath-robes or shawls or the blankets from the foots of their beds; the College did not waste its funds heating the stairwells. Their voices burst around

Vellitt, high and nervous. She snapped out, "Women!" with the authority of long experience, and they fell silent, their anxious, sleep-worn faces tracking her ascent like poppies: the old women they would become for a moment showing through their youth.

There was a circle of space around Jurat's door, the women's curiosity in equipoise with their unwillingness to be associated with whatever crimes she might have committed. Only Therine Angoli had crossed, weeping soundlessly as she held Raba Hust, the Ancient Sarnathian scholar, a heavyset girl with warm brown skin turned the color of ashes and dust in the dim hall light. Hust was Jurat's room-mate. Angoli, Hust, and Jurat had been close, the Three Inseparables.

Vellitt announced to the assembled women, "It remains past curfew. Return to your rooms before the Dean arrives and finds herself obliged to take notice. I need not remind you that discretion is and must always be a byword of Ulthar women. Do not speak of this, even among yourselves, until we know more—especially, to no one outside the College. Miss Hust, I must detain you for another moment."

Without waiting to see her order followed, she disengaged Hust from Angoli's clinging arms and thrust her into the room, to close the door.

~

Jurat and Hust's sitting room was disordered, the wardrobe doors ajar and clothing distributed over every flat surface. Open-faced books teetered in irregular stacks on the paper-strewn floor, and a tray of dirty crockery from the buttery had been shoved halfway beneath one of the two unmade beds. Even the framed prints on the walls, scenic photographic views of the Naraxa Valley from a generation ago, were crooked. The room looked as though it had been ransacked during a particularly violent abduction, but all the women students' rooms did these days—as though there were a fad among them of being as sloppy personally as they were disciplined in their studies.

Hust fell into a padded armchair and, with the heedless flexibility of the young, pulled her feet up, wrapping her arms around her knees and hugging them close to her chest. She was still sobbing.

As Vellitt moved piles of old Articulations from the two wooden study chairs, there was a brisk knock at the door, followed immediately by the entrance of a small woman with short grizzled hair and the clever eye of a hunting bird: Gnesa Petso, the Dean of Ulthar Women's College. She was dressed in a soft woolen robe, once red but a decade old and dimmed by age and laundering.

Without preliminaries, she seated herself on one of the cleared chairs and said briskly, "Hust, every moment is important. What has happened?"

Hust gave her a piece of notepaper, folded twice. The Dean read as Hust said, "When I came back from the library tonight, Jurat wasn't here. That was nine o'clock, I think. She hadn't said anything to me about being out late, but I assumed she had a late pass to be at a lecture or a reading-party, or—" But she was flushed, lying.

The Dean, casting a bright black eye up from the note, said, "Or that she slipped out to be with a man. Miss Hust, do not disgrace yourself trying to sustain someone else's lie."

Hust ducked her head. "I found her letter under my blankets. I've been working on Articulations, so she knew I wouldn't see it until late."

The Dean passed the note to Vellitt. Clarie Jurat's handwriting was as beautiful as everything else about her.

Raba, dear—

Do not be distressed! You know what this says already, don't you— You always see everything so clearly. I go to be with Stephan—I know it is shocking, but there is such an enormous world, and I cannot see it here. He says there are millions of stars, Raba. Millions. *Please show this to*

Therine. I am sorry for the people who will be hurt, but how could I ever explain this to dear old Prof Boe? To the Dean? To my father? *It is impossible—they could not understand—and Stephan tells me it must be tonight or never—and so I go! The greatest adventure, yes? Be happy for me.*

    Your loving,
    Clarie.

The story was soon told. Clarie Jurat had met Stephan Heller when the Three Inseparables had attended a Union debate four weeks ago. He had struck up a conversation outside the Hall, buying them all coffee at the Crévie. He had been captivated by Jurat: no surprise, Hust said—a little wistfully, for of the Inseparables, Raba was the plainest. What *was* a surprise was that Jurat found him equally attractive. He was good-looking, tawny-skinned and dark-eyed with excellent teeth, and very tall (Hust sighed), but it wasn't any of *that*. There was just something *about* him.

The next afternoon, it had been tea for Hust and Jurat—Therine Angoli had been unable to join them because of her Maritime Economic History tutorial—and then it had been Jurat and Stephan, Stephan and Jurat, weeks and weeks of high teas and low teas and tiffins, of walks through Ulthar's quaint narrow streets and punting upon the Aëdl; of after-hour bottles of wine shared in the sorts of public places where the kellarkips did not ask about the University status of young women. That Jurat's studies had not suffered during this month was more a sign of her innate brilliance than of any devotion to her work.

And now this.

The Dean said, "We need to bring her back before this becomes a known thing. Is he a student?" No, Hust rather thought he seemed older than that. "Well, where does he stay? You must know that, yes? She must have said *something.*"

Hust hesitated, biting a cuticle.

Vellitt snapped, "I know you have no wish to break silence, Hust, but believe me: this is the right thing to do. We *must* find her. Do you know who her father is?"

"She never talks about her family. What does it matter, anyway?" Hust dropped her hand, and looked up a little defiantly.

The Dean explained, "Jurat's father is one of the College's Trustees, and he reports to the University's board."

Hust said, "She's a grown woman, and she's in love. She is permitted to plan her own life, surely? What's wrong with that?"

Vellitt snapped, "What's *wrong* is that her father may have the College shut down—"

Hust looked aghast. "Oh, surely not!"

"—and perhaps get women banned from the University altogether," said Vellitt. "*This* is why we must find her quickly and bring her back. Where does he live?"

Hust bit her lip. "I know Heller has been staying at The Speared Hart. He's not from Ulthar. I thought I said: he was special. He's from the waking world. That's where he's taking her."

~

"That *fool*," snarled Vellitt Boe to Gnesa Petso.

It was ten minutes later. The Dean had ordered Hust to return to bed, but Vellitt saw a flicker of a bright shawl above them as they descended the stairwell: Angoli, lurking on the landing. Never mind. Hust would need comfort, and Angoli as well: the Inseparables separated forever now, and for such a reason.

Gnesa and Vellitt had come to Vellitt's rooms as being closer; and she had turned up the gas-jets and poured whiskey for them both. The Fellows of Ulthar Women's College were expected to live disciplined lives free of the indulgences male Fellows of the other colleges might enjoy, but this was honored rather in the breach, even at the best of times. Just now, Vellitt thought they needed the whiskey's bite, but she barely tasted it before she put it down and began pacing.

Gnesa looked up at Vellitt from her seat on one of the worn brocaded settees. "Sit *down*, Vellitt. We must think, and this is not productive."

Vellitt dropped into the facing seat. "I know, but—ah, this is infuriating. I thought we trained our women to think clearly, and this, this elopement— We're always walking a fine line at the best of times. How could she not see that? She could get women banned from the University—and for *what*? For a *whim*?" It was impossible to stay still; she stood to pace again.

"For love," Gnesa said.

Vellitt shook her head. "She is too intelligent not to see the damage—not for her, but for the others, the ones who won't marry, who don't have that option, perhaps. It was selfish. Jurat should be better than that."

"When are young people in love anything but selfish?" said Gnesa. "Were you any better?"

"I harmed no one but myself when I was young," said Vellitt. "And my parents were dead. But—" She bit off the words; took a breath, then a second. "I do see what you are saying, Gnesa. I apologize."

"Accepted," Gnesa said. "So we must find out, *primus*, whether any part of this is true—"

"Jurat may be a fool, but she is no liar."

Gnesa continued, "—*secundus*, whether they have left

Ulthar yet, and if so, *tertius*—the waking world? How does one get there?" Vellitt opened her mouth, but Gnesa raised a finger: "*Primus* first. Go wake up Daekkson and send him to The Speared Hart to see whether they are by some mad chance still there. If so, he can drag her back by the ear and this may be over before dawn. We'll figure out the rest while he's gone."

"I'll rouse him," Vellitt said. "I may as well use some of this energy for *something*."

It took rather less than five minutes to cross the quad, awaken the porter in his rooms behind the main gate, and explain the situation. When Vellitt returned, she found Gnesa had moved to her desk and pushed aside the Articulations clustered there.

"Done," Vellitt said when Gnesa looked up from what she was writing. "He'll report to us here as soon as he returns."

Gnesa nodded. "Excellent. If he does bring her back, there will be little harm done. Provided she's not pregnant, anyway. If she's gone—" She picked up a page before her, half-covered in her precise, crabbed handwriting. "Here's my thinking."

It was a list. Gnesa read it to her, voice raised slightly to be heard from the bedroom as Vellitt dressed. The other Professors and Fellows of Ulthar Women's College would need to be awakened, collected, and told—which meant the scouts would need to be awakened, which meant the housekeeper, who would handle all that. There would have to be an emergency assembly for the students, enjoining silence for all their sakes—they could not count on the news remaining secret within the College; best to take the ram by the horns—and it would have to be before anyone left for lectures and classes. At Matins, then, though there were plenty of students who skipped the rituals. The scouts would need to be told to rouse late-risers to make sure they were there. The kitchen staff would need to be warned that the entire College would be at breakfast in a body right afterward, instead of arriving in their more usual dribs and drabs, or even skipping it altogether.

Gnesa would need to write to Davell Jurat and tell him the College had lost his daughter—"and ask him, *please, kind sir, do not shut us down,*" she said sourly. There would be a different letter to the other Trustees, stating that Jurat had been taken away by a man of the waking world: hinting at unknown sorceries (though certainly not lying directly), so that perhaps the College might not seem so culpable. If everything were handled carefully, and so long as the whole thing could be hushed up, and provided there was no possibility of recurrence, the Trustees might be convinced not to close the College.

Vellitt walked out to the sitting room buttoning her

walking skirt, as Gnesa ended, "If they *were* at the inn but are gone now, find her somehow." Gnesa looked up. "This is all assuming that he is what he says he is, a dreamer, and not just some smooth-talking Thran man, here to seduce University girls."

Vellitt sat to lace her shoes. "I don't think so. Jurat has read Maths with me for three years now. The students tell their tutors things—you know how they do. I know she's ignored men who were much more handsome than this Stephan Heller sounds. Hust said he was special, and I think he is. There's a . . . sheen to waking-world men. A dark charisma. If you spend more than an hour or two with one, it's obvious. *That's* what Jurat was responding to."

The Dean put down the pen and leaned back, eyeing the painting of Irem above the desk. "Too bad. It would be better for us if he *were* a charlatan: then we could track him, eventually anyway. Otherwise— What if he has taken her back to his world already, Vellitt? I know dreamers can leave our lands from anywhere. They vanish when they awaken in their own world. I saw it once, a few years back—a man walking along Dubv Lane, and then he was gone."

Vellitt said, "Stephan Heller could do that, but Clarie can't. *This* is her world; she's awake already. I think they will have to pass through a Gate. There's one on Hatheg-

Kla. Dreamers call it the Gate of Deeper Slumber but it just looks ordinary, just wrought iron and moss. There are supposed to be stairs behind it that lead to a temple serving the Flame, and another Gate, and then the waking world."

Gnesa was eying her, surprised.

Vellitt added, reluctantly, "I knew a dreamer, a long time ago. Let me show you something, Gnesa." She picked up *Aldrovandi on Theoretical Geometry* from the seat under the gabled window, and riffled the monograph's pages until she found what she sought and handed it to the Dean.

It was a piece of card-stock a little larger than her hand, printed with a vivid photographic image of an unfamiliar town square: pale stone buildings and light gray slate flagstones, white umbrellas, glowing green trees, crowds of people dressed in bright colors. Where the sky should be was a flat blueness.

Gnesa looked up. "Is this somewhere in Carcassone?"

"Not Carcassone. He always said our Carcassone was named for a place in his own world, but it's not that, either. Look: different buildings, and the colors everyone is wearing. This is the waking world. It's a place there." She pointed to words along the bottom: *Avignon, la Place de l'Horloge.*

"Where is the sky?" Gnesa touched the blueness with

one short finger.

"That blue *is* their sky."

"There is no patterning, no mass? What is it made of?" Gnesa's field was Material Studies. She turned the card over and fell silent. The back was simpler: CARTE POSTALE printed in dark blue on plain white; angular handwriting in ink that had faded from black to the color of old blood.

Veline, you always wish for proofs—R.

"'Veline'?"

"Me." Vellitt looked down at the little photograph, the tiny bright women, the specks on the piazza's flagstones: birds, or debris. "I didn't believe him when he told me about the sky, so he brought this to me. Gnesa, I can follow Jurat and Stephan Heller to Hatheg-Kla. I know the way. I've crossed the forest and I've seen the Gate."

Gnesa frowned. "Too dangerous. If it comes to that, I'll send Daekkson."

"It must be me."

"No. Daekkson is twenty years younger than you—and, not inconsequentially, male. The west . . . that is rough country, Vellitt."

Vellitt snorted "The Skai plains? Hardly!— No, I do take your point, but consider: which of us is more likely to bring her back? I'm her tutor, Arbitrix for her Exams. We need her to *listen,* to understand what is at risk if she clings to this folly. If he comes up with Jurat on the road to the Gate, she will not listen to him. Stephan Hellar may make trouble—if he loves her, he *will* do so. It will be hard for Daekkson to retrieve her without a scandal. And if they have passed it? He has no options."

"Would *you* have options?" said Gnesa.

"More than Daekkson, anyway. Trust me, Gnesa. I will find a way."

Gnesa stared into the flames for a moment. "Your point is valid, and I accede. But—can you travel fast enough?"

"I'll have to, won't I?"

They were interrupted by a knock at the door. Daekkson, back from The Speared Hart: Stephan Heller had departed that very afternoon in the company of an extraordinarily beautiful woman: obviously Jurat, by the nightkip's dazzled description. They had asked about roads leading west.

Gnesa dismissed Daekkson and turned to Vellitt. "That's that, then. Are you sure you want to do this?"

"Does it matter?" Vellitt said, suddenly tired of it all. "It's what I do: teach women not to be fools. I have spent the last twenty years of my life here—making a place for women who don't fit anywhere else. She *can't* be allowed to ruin it for the others."

"All right. How soon will you depart?"

"Immediately. Professor Freser at Thanes-College can take my lectures and students. Can you let everyone else know who needs to?"

"Done." Gnesa jotted something down and stood. "I'll get the Bursar to pull together some funds for you. Bring Jurat back to us, Vellitt. And yourself." Gnesa embraced her, a sudden surprising touch, then was gone.

~

It was not quite an immediate departure, but it was quick for all that. Vellitt Boe unearthed from the recesses of her closet a small leather pack, crumpled and smelling slightly, pleasingly, of ancient rains and distant soil. She found her old walking boots and her walking stick of gnurled black wood.

When Vellitt Boe was young, she had been a far-traveller, a great walker of the Six Kingdoms, which waking-world men called the dream lands. She had seen Irem, that pillared ruin, and she knew that it was not the fantasia of the Academician's pretty painting above her desk but—like the rest of the world—dirtier and infinitely more interesting.

She had been born in the harbor town of Jaren, where the frigid Xari spilled into the northern reaches of the Cerenarian Sea; but in her nineteenth year she left, and for years after that she voyaged: crossed plains and forests and fenlands; ascended mountains and walked in the belly of the under-realms; sailed in strange-hulled boats across unfamiliar oceans under the low sky. She had travelled until she realized that this yearning life could not be sustained, that time would eventually erode away her strength and courage; and so she stopped. She applied to the Women's College of the University of Celephaïs and settled into rooms there, a perfect student, brilliant and disciplined. She received her Physical Studies degree in Mathematics and came to Ulthar, to stay and grow old and teach other young women more rational responses to their restlessness. It had been sensible, a reasonable end to her far-travelling youth.

Packing came to her automatically, a memory stained not into her mind but into the muscles of her hands and arms. The tricks came back: how to roll her spare socks and where the tin box of medical supplies best fit. She stowed a sweater, a blouse, heavy gloves, her flat steel canteen, a comb and toothbrush, soap in a small bottle, whetstone and oil, matches—all the oddments of travelling finding their places in the pack as though they knew their way. She added her electric torch, but such torches had existed only as expensive, temperamental fripperies thirty years ago, so she also found her old tinder-box. She tested the flint: satisfied, for her hand had preserved the precise, economical flick that sent blue-white sparks spattering across her leather desk-pad. Dropping the tinder-box into its little interior pocket, she lifted the rucksack by its shoulder straps. It was lighter than it would have been, for she no longer had rope and grapnel, nor her blanket roll, nor the compact little cooking kit she had once carried; but it was heavy enough, for all that.

She carried it out to the sitting room and dropped it on the settee. She still owned the machete she had carried so long ago, so she unearthed it from the back of a drawer and strapped the ancient sheath in its place. It nestled gently into the cradle it had worn for itself, just beneath the top flap.

It was only a few days' travel, in any case. She would be crossing the plains of the River Skai, going through Nir and Hatheg-town—small but civilized enough in their way. Later, when she approached the wastelands of the Stony Desert, there would be roadside inns, or a farmer could be paid for a night in an unused or hastily vacated bedroom. It would be more dangerous when she entered the forest that girdled Hatheg-Kla, for it was inhabited by the zoogs, strange, sinuous, and untrustworthy; but she would be less than a day under those glowing trees, and she had been there before. As for the waking world, if it should come to that? She had no idea what to expect, so there was no predicting what would be needed.

She took up her knife from where it had rested for twenty years, a combination paperweight and letter-opener half-buried beneath the papers on her desk. It made a tiny sound as she unsheathed it. The edge was still sharp. She returned it to its sheath and slipped it beneath her jacket.

She laced on her walking boots and stood, and for a moment looked about herself, at the dark, crooked gables and slanting ceilings of her rooms, the cluttery wallpaper and soft furniture. She had been in these rooms for twenty years and everything was as known as her own reflection: more, for in recent years she had not lingered on that ageing stranger in the silvered glass.

On an impulse, she walked into the bedroom and looked at herself in the pier mirror. A stranger infinitely familiar stared back: a stern-eyed woman in walking tweeds, with heavy laced boots and black-and-silver hair pulled away from her lined face. An old woman but not soft—or, she thought with a sudden inward wry laugh, perhaps not quite *old*, but also softer than she had been.

She was interrupted by a soft knock: the College's Bursar, with academic robes tossed over her seafoam-green nightdress and her hair a tangled braid, looking quite mad. She had things for Vellitt: letters of credit, an oiled-leather purse filled with coins, a small parcel of weight-stamped gold lozenges, and a little notebook ruled for bookkeeping. She did not speak of Vellitt's task, only said a quick farewell, with a stern enjoinder to record all expenditures for the University's Accountancies. As the Bursar left, a sleepy scullery maid appeared, bringing sandwiches from the kitchen for the first day's travel. Typical of Gnesa to think of this, even in the middle of so much else to do.

~

And so Vellitt Boe left Ulthar Women's College, walking silent and alone across the quad and through the postern gate: Daeksson back at his post in the porter's hutch, looking uncommonly weary. "Well forth," he said as she passed; and, "No ill thing," she replied. Stepping through the postern gate, she let the heavy door fall shut behind her.

She paused and looked about herself. A narrow slice of sky overhead showed as pitch darkness, for the lane was narrow here, ancient and kenneled and crowded close by stone walls pierced by many-paned windows, dark now.

This was Tierce Lane, but she knew them all, every mews and alley. For twenty years she had paced Ulthar's bounds, traversed its parks and ancient greens, crossed squares, passed fountains. And the people: her colleagues and Fellows and friends—and a thousand lesser connections, with kellarkips and shopkips, the girl who served sardines and cream tea at Gulserene's and the cheerful delivery boy from Patles's Books. These were home, or something that passed for home.

She was brought back to herself by a sudden movement at her feet. It was the small black cat that had followed her to Clarie Jurat's rooms; or another like it. It wreathed her ankles, gazing upward, and its eyes shone with light reflected from the lamp over the postern gate. "I have nothing for you," Vellitt said. "Go back inside, little one."

It did not. Vellitt walked to where Tierce Lane met the High and turned west, and the cat trotted beside her. This was the old part of town: half-timbered buildings with overhung second stories and peaked roofs, the occasional shrine or public building of heavy granite or blocks of labradorite. The air smelled of ancient mold, but also of herbs, of rue and basil and catmint, for every window had a hanging basket bright with greenery. When she crossed Affleur Road, a single lamp shone in the Weeping Tower of New College—a student in his rooms, cramming for Exams as Clarie Jurat should have been. Later, on the Mercü, a light beamed from the open back door of a bakery: the smell of fresh bread everywhere. There were few other signs of life; even Ulthar's ubiquitous cats were scarce, pursuing their private errantries as the night eased into dawn.

She crossed Six Corners, automatically making the El-der Sign. After this, the High widened and opened into a series of arcades and markets, and the smells changed, to new-gathered greens, spices, hanging pheasants, and the pork and mutton that already hung in linen-wrapped pink slabs in front of the flescher's; for now morning was coming. The tea-seller called out a greeting to Vellitt as she unlaced her canvas shop-front; they had talked often enough of tea, weather, far places. Vellitt only waved as she passed. If all went well she would be back soon; if it did not— But there was no reason to think of that.

She turned onto Nir Road, and the buildings spaced themselves out, became detached houses, then cottages with gardens. Small hornless goats eyed her through withy fences. She heard poultry chuckling in back gar-dens, and once through the open window of an ivy-wrapped cottage, a woman's voice singing: *"Sarnath, Sarkomand, Khem, and Toldees; Always say, 'Thank you!' and, 'Sir, if you please.'"*

Vellitt paused when she came to the top of Never-rye Hill, panting a little from the long ascent. Ulthar behind her was achingly beautiful in the rose-pink rays of the new sun: the Six Hills crazed as a tumbled quilt, a ran-dom patchwork of red gabled roofs frilled with ornamental iron chimney-pots and lightning rods, and the dark gaps that were roads and gardens. Crowning the highest of the hills, the Temple: a tower surrounded by a grassy field, bright with the first tents for the great Sheep-fair, which was to commence in three days. Like a garland about the hill's base were the Seven Colleges of Ulthar's University: New College, Eb-Taqar, and Meianthe School and the others; ancient, cool, palladian structures of pale stone blushing the sunrise pink of cherry blossoms, their quadrangles turned trapezoidal by perspective; hints of lush garden. Newest and humblest of them, the Women's College was a clutter of buildings scarce fancier than the town, but she gazed hungrily until she identified the bell tower and the slate roof of the new dining hall.

Never-rye Hill was capped with a little shrine, knee-high and fashioned of porphyry so worn that it was impossible to know what god it honored, whether Great One or Other or some being altogether different. It was traditional to leave a nut when one left Ulthar, and the shrine was half-buried in hazels and almonds, walnuts and acorns, everything much picked over by squirrels. She had forgotten to bring an offering, but a century ago, some thoughtful traveller had planted a walnut tree close by. It took but a moment to find a fallen nut in the long grasses and lay it among the others.

The small black cat from the College had seated itself upon the shrine's stained offering slab (for it was not always nuts that were offered here) and was cleaning its ears with complete absorption. It was unlike cats to travel like this, but she also knew that cats lived according to their own schemes and agendas. "It grows harder from here," she warned the cat, but it dropped to the path and walked forward as though to say, *You are wasting time.*

Vellitt came to the great stone bridge that crossed the River Skai and paid the penny toll to cross. She inquired of the money-taker whether she remembered two people from the night before, but the girl only shook her head: her brother had managed the booth; she had only begun her shift an hour ago. "People mostly don't cross at night, any case," she added with a melodramatic shiver, "on account of the ghost!"—set to launch into the story of the man buried alive in the bridge's masonry. But Vellitt had heard it before and moved on, leaving the girl to relate it to the reluctant zebra-drover behind her.

Her plan was to follow the Lhosk-Hatheg road past Hatheg-town, to the great curve where it approached the zoogs' forest, just before it plunged into the Stony Desert to meet the caravan road. For now, she was still on the plains of the Skai: open country threaded through with hedges, pretty rolling farmland, and pasturage the dusty green of late summer, scattered with white-fleeced sheep.

She stopped for lunch at an inn well past the bridge, and afterward, she repacked her rucksack, to remove everything that four hours' walk made less imperative, arranging to have the excess shipped back to College. The black cat watched with interest, and when Vellitt at last shrugged back into the straps, it leapt easily onto the top flap and settled there. It almost exactly countered the weight she had just removed, but its breath was pleasant on her ear. It seemed a fair trade.

The afternoon was slower: she had always been a great walker, but it had been years since she had gone so far. Being sensible about her age, she had called it, but in fact there had been no impetus to work harder when she was only traversing the mannerly Karthian Hills or the pleasant garden-lands of the Skai. Her muscles stretched and grew warm, began to ache and then grew numb: all usual enough for the first day out, she recalled.

The air was misted with pollen from the ripening fields. Across a valley, she saw (and heard) a tractor trundling across a pasture, a glossy, violent red against all the green, but mechanical vehicles were still a recent and rare thing in these regions, and mostly it was oxen or zebras pulling carts and threshers, and the voices of the drivers calling out, *Chirac, chirac, hai!* The sun blanked the sky to a pale blue, the titanic swellings faded to no more than slight differences in tint and texture.

She stopped for the night just past the little town of Nir, at a road-inn called the Lost Lamb. No one there had seen Jurat and Stephan Heller. The only other travellers were three young traders with cinnamon and sandalwood from distant Oonai, on their way to the thousand gilded spires of Thran. They smelled of their sweet wares, and she could not help but breathe deeply; but they, seeing only an old woman in sturdy shoes, did not speak to her.

~

Vellitt Boe awoke aching in every joint. For the first miles, all she could think of were hot baths and her research desk back at the University library, no doubt delightfully baking in the sunlight that would be coming through the clerestory windows; but her stiffness eased with movement, and she began to walk as the far-traveller she had once been. Certainly, the morning was beautiful, the sun bright and the seething sky faded to faint basketweaves. As she left the plains and ascended into the hills, the farmhouses and cottages became less frequent, and their fences had the look of being constructed to keep things *out* as much as *in*. The hedgerows grew wild, and sometimes she caught hints of a green glow in their tangled hearts.

She came to the top of a ridge and saw the country spread around her: the Lhosk-Hatheg Road a pale line across the tangled green and gold countryside; the peaks and the green wooded slopes of Mount Lerion to her north and white-capped Mount Thurai to the northwest; and to the west, hazy with distance and always so much larger than she ever remembered, the great mountain Hatheg-Kla, its snowy peak fading into the shifting sky, so that she could not be sure of its final height.

She stopped at a remote house and bought bread, tomatoes, and slices of smoked goat's belly. Vellitt asked about Jurat and Stephan Heller, but the farm-woman had seen nothing, only took the money unsmiling and returned inside, shutting the door firmly against the slight midday breeze. Vellitt lunched alone a mile later, on the parapet of a stone bridge across the sun-spangled Reffle. Knowing the stream's reputation, she did not refill her canteen, and when the cat ambled down to investigate the water's edge, she called it back. A moment later her caution proved justified: a bird alighting on a willow wand that overhung the Reffle dropped suddenly, as though dead or drugged, and a red-scaled carp the size of a wild boar rose from the shadows of the stream bottom and sucked the bird in.

The afternoon was less pleasant: hotter and dusty. Her shoulders under the straps felt raw, and her thighs burned. Just before dusk she stopped at a farmhouse to rent a room from a grim-faced man who answered direct questions but offered nothing more. Yeh, Hatheg was just a'ways along t'road. Yeh, he saw a couple walking that way this very morn: the girl swart-haired and the man very tall. Yeh, he might've been a dreamer (he made the Elder Sign); he had that look on 'm; but he wasn't paying no attention, he had his own work to do, not idle like some. That night in the little attic room, Vellitt wrote Gnesa Petso: *I'm relieved, I suppose,* she ended. *I might have been wrong, and Jurat on a dhow down the Skai, halfway to the coast.*

The third day started worse still: everything sore and a new, searing pain in her right heel where a blister had broken. When she came to Hatheg-town, she posted her letter and purchased food but did not tarry, and by midmorning she had come far enough that she saw a faint viridian glow on the scattered clouds in the north, light reflected from the glowing fungi of the zoogs' forest.

Past Hatheg, the road became a mere track. There were no people and no roadhouses or farms, but many tangled, shrubby copses; rangeland a-haze with pollen and insects; weed fields that raised guerdons of flame-red blooms as high as her head. The green in the clouds grew brighter, and coming over a hill in the early afternoon, she saw the forest's edge to the north. The line between the rangeland and the glowing woodland looked so precise that it seemed almost to have been ruled by the Elder Ones.

She turned onto the next track that headed north. It was wide enough for carts but had fallen into disuse, and it ended a few miles later in the weed-choked yard of a ruined, crumbling grange, home only to dust and spiders. Vellitt walked to the well, but the reservoir was dry, and she thought better of trying the rusted iron pump. It would, she suspected, be shriekingly loud in this silent place. After a short search, she found a narrow path leading toward the forest, and followed it.

Zoogs were small, essentially cowards that would not threaten humans unless they felt they could get away with it; but she had no wish to test the limits of their cowardice, so in late afternoon she stopped a half-mile from the forest's edge at what must once have been a shepherd's close. The high, tight-folded stone walls were still largely intact, thick and taller than Vellitt, with a single narrow entrance through which sheep had been driven. When she climbed a broken section, she found the stone remains of a shepherd's seat that overlooked the area around the close. She made a pad from her raincloak and settled in, her electric torch and machete close at hand. It was surprisingly comfortable.

Cats move fearlessly between the dream lands, the

moon, and the waking world—and to other, unknowable places—but this cat was no fool. It stayed close to Vellitt, and as night deepened it climbed into her lap and would not leave. "You should have considered all this before you came," Vellitt said, and her voice surprised her. It had been midmorning since she had heard any human sound.

She could not tell if it understood her. In her far-travelling days, Vellitt had known a dreamer who claimed to understand the speech of cats, but of all the cats she had ever met in Ulthar—a town crammed with them—none had ever spoken to her, nor to anyone else; none that she knew, anyway. The dreamer had been a serious-minded man and dishonesty had not been his besetting flaw, so perhaps it was a waking-world thing.

Time passed. As night fell, the forest's viridian glow grew stronger, but this was the darkest sky she had seen in decades. She could see every constellation, every star. As well as she could recall from her schoolgirl lessons, she recited their names: Algol, Gemma, Arcturus, Mizar; the blue spark of Polaris; green-mantled Venus; the red disk of Mars, large enough that her outstretched thumb just covered it. Ninety-seven stars in the dream-realms sky; six constellations.

Clarie Jurat had written, *He says there are millions of stars.* Vellitt had heard this before about the waking world, but she could not imagine it. Where would they all fit? The sky was hardly infinite: she could see its pendulous, titanic folds, its shifting patterns, black on black. And if each planet or star had its own buffeting, fretful, whimsical god, how could the waking world survive?

And so the night passed and always Vellitt's face turned to the scant stars and the moonless, massy sky beyond. Once she heard sounds, so faint that she wondered at first whether they were real, of long-toed paws pushing through grass, fluttering whispers. She turned on her electric torch and cast the homely yellow beam down into the grasses around the close. Silence fell suddenly. She was not disturbed again.

~

Vellitt Boe did sleep, though she had not intended it, and awoke to a coruscating sky turned rose-pink by the sunrise. She continued along the narrow path. The cat remained with her, hunched on her pack so that she felt the tickle of its whiskers against her jaw. When she turned her face, she saw its eyes glowing leaf-green and intent.

The wall of underbrush that marked the forest margins thinned and was replaced by a thick mold underfoot, the rotting remains of the dead leaves that had fallen from the vast and towering oaks crowding everywhere. Young oaks pushed through the mold, as did ferns of surprising size and pale-domed mushrooms several feet across. The tree trunks were wound with ivy or ruffled with shelf-like fungi climbing as high as she could see, to where the oaks' groping boughs tangled into a canopy. The leaves blocked the sun except as a mottled glow, but the forest was light enough, from the green shadowless luminescence emitted by the fungi. The air was clammy and smelled of decay.

She remembered how to read the patterns the fungi made, and found her way to what passed for a zoog highway. She had a password she had learned long ago and she spoke it at intervals, though the noises did not come easily to her tongue, and she was not sure it would work after so many years. Though she did not see the zoogs, she heard them sometimes, just at the edges of what she could detect: the pattering of their narrow paws among the ferns, or a rustling that might have been mistaken for a breeze (save that there was none), and several times, the fluttering sounds of their whispered speech. The black cat crouched tight-muscled and unmoving on her pack. The zoogs would not have frightened her much when she was younger, but now . . . And yet, why? *They* were not changed, and, while she was older, neither had she altered in any fundamental way. Perhaps she had grown wiser with age.

After a time, the highway branched and, recognizing

her location, she took the right-hand path, coming at last to a clearing around a mighty slab of stone set into the forest floor: an access point to the under-realms fashioned by gugs in eons past. The zoogs feared it and would not approach, which made it a safe place to pause, provided the great slab did not lift.

Vellitt knew something of the under-realms from her far-travelling youth. It had been an accidental horror to fall through a sinkhole in the Mnar swamps with her companion. At first, she would not have survived it without his knowledge, for he had alliances among the ghouls—slumping canine-faced creatures that ate the dead and were said to have secret routes into all worlds. He enlisted their aid in returning to the surface, and taught Vellitt bits of their glibbering, meeping speech. But the party was attacked by ghasts—scabrous, humped, horse-like; with flat faces and unsettling, intelligent eyes—and she had been separated from the rest of them. After endless dark whiles finding her way alone, she came to a city of gugs: enormous six-pawed monsters with vertical mouths framed by shining red eyes on stalks. Eventually she found a party of ghouls to whom she spoke in her limited way, and they brought her back to her companion. When they at last emerged, the sun had blinded her for hours. She had been underground for nearly a month.

Vellitt ate and rested beside the great slab, and began again her long walk through the high-ceilinged tunnels of twisted wood. The zoogs returned to haunt her steps, and now she felt as though there were a purpose to their stalking. The password had not worked after all: too old, or perhaps the zoogs no longer cared what might happen if they failed to honor it. They paced her beneath the ferns and mushrooms and in the branches overhead. At times, small loathsome paws reached out to brush her ankles or back. Their flutterings sounded excited, even to her unaccustomed ears.

Feeling like a fool, she drew the machete from its sheath; but perhaps she did not look like one, for the zoogs pulled back. Beyond the canopy, daylight was ending, but she was too far into the forest to retreat. It never grew truly dark, though the viridian glow was like corpse-light, faint and slightly sickening to her eyes. Her electric torch's batteries would not last the night, so she fashioned a flambeau from a fallen branch and the contents of a small bottle of pitch she carried, grateful to find the skill remained.

She walked. The zoogs began pressing her again, but with sweeps of the torch she kept pushing them back. There seemed to be scores of them, never fully to be seen: glimpses of brown fur among the ferns, a prehensile tail zipping from sight, yellow eyes gleaming out at her from hidden places. Her arms grew tired. The cat growled steadily, barely audible.

A young zoog, bolder than its fellows, crept close and nipped her ankle. Unthinking, she swung the machete, which connected with a meaty sensation that ran from her hand into her shoulder. The zoog fell back with a panicking, quavering howl entirely unlike its fluttering language. Again, the zoogs retreated and she pressed forward. Again, they overcame their fear and crowded close. They were hunting her.

And Vellitt found that, despite her exhaustion and her age, she could run. She threw the torch toward a zoog that approached too nearly, and fled forward by the green light: the cat afoot and running, a fluid shadow just ahead. She knew where she was, for she passed a standing stone she remembered from years past, ancient, hexagonal, and pierced. She was close now, but the zoogs seemed to know her goal, as well. Several had climbed into the trees ahead of her and were waiting to drop on her. She shouted, "Go on then, you!"—her voice breathless and hoarse with anger—and as she ran beneath them, she raised the machete over her head. They chose instead to drop behind her and join the pursuing band.

The overhanging trees opened out as she ran into a clearing: a quarter-moon and the looming shadow of the mountain Hatheg-Kla against the black starred sky—and on moss-thick flagstones stood the gates, a free-standing basalt trilithon framing paired portals of black iron. For the first time she doubted herself, for only once before this had she seen the Gate of Deeper Slumber, and then it had been ajar; and now the gates were closed and might be locked.

The zoogs poured into the clearing behind her, and for the first time she could see them clearly: scores of brown, shadowy forms with long, articulate limbs, knee-high as they loped on all fours. Their forward-looking hunters' eyes shone yellow as they raced toward her.

The cat streaked through a gap in the iron; and Vellitt following slammed into the portal with a deep ringing noise, as though someone had struck a gong the size of a city. At the immense sound the zoogs stopped short and with cries of fear tumbled backward into the trees. Vellitt tore open a gate—unlocked after all—and passed onto a broad staircase of pale moss-covered stone. She ran to the first landing and there halted at last. The zoogs did not follow her. She was, perhaps, safe.

~

It took a long while to catch her breath, and before her heart had stopped pounding, her sweat had turned icy on her face and under her breasts and arms. The cat crouched beside her, panting in its small-lunged way, so she poured water into the canteen's cap, and the cat lapped it dry while she drained the rest. Her right ankle hurt viciously, and she bled in a dozen places from scratches caused by tearing through the branches. She had not known she could run so far—or at all—but as a young woman she had been quick and strong, and some of that remained.

She looked about. The zoogs' forest was not visible except as a glow that seemed to come from a great distance, much farther below than the steps she had ascended. From this side, the trilithon was the same rough-cut basalt, but the gates were not iron: one, elaborately carved of a single piece of ivory cut from some unknown but mammoth beast; the other, woven of broad strips of translucent horn. If she walked through those gates, would she find herself in yet another place, *her* dream lands? Did women have dream lands? In all her far-travelling, she had never seen a woman of the waking world nor heard of one, but she thought of the little picture card of *Avignon, la Place de l'Horloge,* the town square and all its women in their bright summer dresses. There were as many women as men in that image: was that even possible?

Finally her exhaustion caught up with her: days of walking and only an hour or so of sleep in the past two.

Vellitt dropped into something that was nearly a coma. If she dreamed, she remembered nothing of it.

She woke to full daylight. Her arms hurt from holding the torch and machete, and her ankle had swollen, but otherwise she felt amazingly well, alive as she had not in years. She smiled, remembering something a travelling companion had said long ago: *Nothing like not dying to make you feel alive.* Hungry as she was, she ate nothing, for she would have no more water until she came to the temple.

Curled close beside Vellitt's pack, the cat slept on. It had found its own meal, for there were bloody paw-prints upon the railing, and tufts of fur the greasy brown of a young zoog's pelt: impressive, for she would not have thought the cat was large enough for such prey. Only when Vellitt shouldered her pack did the cat stretch lengthily, blinking its vivid eyes against the morning sun. "Would you like a ride?" she asked and bent low, but it only leapt to the railing and trotted upward on its own.

She had been told that the stairs between the Gate and the temple of Flame were seven hundred in number, but she quickly lost count. The stairs hairpinned up forested crags so steep that she could reach out and touch the rock as she ascended, for the stairs soon became no more than irregular granite ledges interposed with steep pitches of trail. She climbed beyond the tree line, until there were no living things but Vellitt and the cat, which, against the nature and character of its kind, was systematically picking its way up the mountain. She still could not see Hatheg-Kla's uppermost reaches, only soaring cliffs fading against the pale patterns of the heavy-swelling sky.

Her muscles were aflame, and she labored for each wheezing breath. The air was thinner here, and it smelled different, as though spiced by strange seas, ice fields immeasurably distant; and she wondered whether this were the smell of the waking world, or whether the scent was from space itself. Was she still *in* her world? When she paused for breath, as she often found herself forced to do, she saw behind her only an ocean of clouds eye-achingly bright in the sunlight, and overhead, the sky's faint, coruscating anthemions.

Not seven hundred steps but what seemed thousands, yet there was eventually an end to them. It had been a long time since she had looked up; her head was bent to watch her feet, focused on the next step and the next and the next, running with sweat until she ran out of moisture and it dried to salt on her skin. And suddenly there were no more steps and she raised her head.

She stood on a granite ledge some twenty paces across and twice that long, smooth as a lecture-hall floor and glittering with quartzite. To one side the world fell away into the cloud-fields she had climbed through, and the moiréed sky, so close it seemed she might almost reach out and touch some coil of that mutable substance. To the other side was a concave rock face pierced everywhere with windows and doors and little balconies carved of living rock. A hundred feet over her head, the rock face bulged out, sheltering the ledge from the sun.

She was still catching her breath when she saw a man in one of the upper windows. Perceiving her, he vanished, reappearing a moment later upon a stone balcony to descend a ladder, which he managed nimbly despite the voluminous draperies of his violet-colored robes and the laced sandals upon his feet. He was civil to the cat but disdainful to her, though he could not do less than the ancient laws of the temple demanded, showing her to a guest-cave and sending for food, water, and wine. She asked for news of the dreamer Stephan Heller and his companion: whether they lingered here or had passed already into the waking world—or had, perhaps, not yet arrived—but he would say nothing. He could not disregard her application for an audience with the temple's priests, but he heard her with little courtesy and left immediately.

She drank water until sweat finally broke out, then ate. Her cave was cold, glaring with light that streamed through a large opening high in one wall; but she slept as well as ever she had in her gabled rooms in Ulthar.

~

For the next two days, she waited in growing frustration. She sent messages to the high priests Nasht and Kaman-Thah via the disdainful acolyte assigned to attend her, and by every other violet-robed man she saw, priest or proselyte. She gave her name but did not speak of the College, nor of her status as a professor of the University, for she knew that away from the garden-lands of the world, there was often little notion of educating women. Otherwise there was nothing she could do. She learned on the first day that she was the only guest.

She filled her hours. She paced on the polished ledge watching the sky shift, picotage blurring into strange foliation and congeries of fracturing cubes; trying, as she always did, to understand the underlying rules. Since it was not forbidden, she also explored the honeycombed caves of the temple. Many of the corridors and rooms were torchlit, smelling of pitch and sweet resins, but there were deeper, less travelled tunnels, illuminated only by lichens that glowed a dull, cool brown; and once, a sickly pink that caused an immediate and intense headache that lasted for hours.

Late the first afternoon, she found a long room lit by a row of windows high upon one wall. There were dark paintings on the walls, glass-faced cabinets, and tall shelves stacked with scrolls and hand-books. She took down a small scroll, written in a script she recognized as Ib'n, which meant it was unimaginably ancient; and indeed the vellum (if that is what it was) cracked as she held it merely from the pressure of her fingers. She replaced it carefully, and took instead a hand-book bound in dun-colored buckram with strange words on its cover: DANIEL DEFOE MOLL FLANDERS. They meant nothing, so she flipped the book open—it was her own language; the strange words were names—and she realized it was a book from the waking world. She looked more carefully: many of the books were similarly alien, and inside the cabinets were unfamiliar objects of steel or brass or a bright glossy substance like lacquer. She reopened the book and began to read, but an aged man in violet robes so old they had faded to lavender entered the room and castigated her for touching the books. Despite the differences in language, age, and sex, his tone was a mirror of that of Uneshyl Pos, the librarian at the Women's College; for all librarians are the same librarian.

On the second day, Vellitt found herself near the cavern of Flame itself—she could hear a rich, roaring crackling and see light of an inconstant bloody red flickering at the far end of a tunnel—but she was turned aside by a severe-looking man with a great forked red beard, who had something of grandness in his manner and bore beaded crimson gloves upon his hands. He turned away, but she laid her hand on his arm and spoke. "Please. I am seeking two people, a dreamer from the waking world, and one of our own, a young woman of Ulthar. Can you at least tell me whether they passed this way?" The priest looked at her hand as though deciding whether to push it off, but said nothing, and she persisted: "I have a duty to retrieve my charge, Clarie Jurat. I cannot go without knowing whether she has passed through here."

She thought he gave a start at the name, but he replied only, "I will tell you this: no one of the temple has opened the Gate, not in many years."

She was not unaccustomed to rhetorical evasions, so she asked a little tartly, "Then, has anyone else?"

But the man said only, "This part of the temple is forbidden," and left her. She watched his back, receding, rigid with disapproval. She toyed with the notion of defying him—and indeed, the young woman she had been might have done so, trusting she would not be caught; at the worst, that the priests would not kill her—but she was older and could no longer trust to youth or beauty to get her out of trouble. And wiser: there was no point to such defiance.

She turned at random down another corridor and found herself in a high-ceilinged chamber filled with a gentle white light. The lovely cavern had all the appearance of a secret garden, for on its floor were green mosses like grass, spangled with colonies of mold like starry white flowers; it was these that illuminated the space. Tall, heavy-stiped fungoids trailed hyphae, elegant as willow wands, and beneath them were things that looked like bright-leafed aloes, though as she approached she saw that they were fungi, as well. The scent reminded her of lilies but was not; the slight strangeness was not unpleasant.

A broad pillar rose at the cavern's center, pierced with a gate caked so thickly with lichens that she could not identify the figures wrought into the iron, except that they were creatures. Inside the pillar was a staircase of white stone, circling upward into shadow. The cat (which had accompanied her for its own inscrutable reasons) loped forward, squeezed through a gap in the gate, and trotted up the stairs. Vellitt placed her hand on the iron, but the metal burned as though it had been newly pulled from a fire, and she stepped back quickly.

She was returning to her rooms when a purple-robed boy found her, panting like a dog in summertime from running. "Nasht has called for you," he gasped, and all but dragged her by the hand. She followed him, wondering whether she was to be cast from the temple at last. The boy trotted ahead, looking back every few feet, but she refused to rush. She would not meet the high priest

Nasht sweaty and breathless.

They came to tall doors of white wood bound in iron. The boy effaced himself; wordlessly, the two acolytes standing sentry opened the doors. She stepped forward and found herself in a long, narrow audience room, lined with statues of unsettling configuration and dimly illuminated by sconced torches burning every shade of red: crimson, scarlet, and carmine. Raised on a many-stepped dais of polished basalt at the room's far end were two seats as grand as thrones, and over each hung an immense boulder of black granite that glittered with reflected flames. The left-hand seat was empty, but a black-bearded man sat on the other, wearing heavy robes of indigo and violet, and bearing on his head a pshent studded with opals. She stepped forward.

The High Priest looked down at her and exclaimed, "Veline!" in a voice that summoned a memory she could not quite grasp.

She looked curiously up at him. "Not for many years. I am Vellitt Boe of Ulthar. I come for news of Clarie Jurat, and to retrieve her if I can."

The man stood, so that his pshent brushed the overhanging boulder. Something in the manner of his movement plucked at that lost memory.

"Reon?" she said, hesitantly.

~

Recognition changed things. The High Priest Nasht, who once had been Reon Atescre, led her from the red-lit audience room through a door behind the thrones to a small windowless cave, stone-walled, low-ceilinged, and furnished with surprising attention to comfort. Spots of light from the many pierced-work lanterns spangled across the plush wall tapestries, the heavy padded furniture, and the shelves stacked with novels and pastoral poetry: a room at odds with the severity of the temple as a whole.

He poured glasses of the sweet green wine of Hap, and they sat looking at one another for a moment. Reon Atescre of Sona Nyl had been slim and laughing-eyed, a lighthearted, fearless man who was not attracted to women, seeing her for what she was and not what he wanted her to be, and therefore an easy companion to her. They had parted ways in the infamous demon-city Thalarion for no reason but the restlessness that is in the young; in all the years since, she had heard nothing of how he fared. Now, so changed, and heavier altogether: his face nearly hidden behind his black, spade-shaped beard, so that she could not see his mobile mouth. His light step had turned ponderous with weight and authority. Even his voice seemed heavier, its humor silted away.

"I have had a vision, but first I'll answer the question you've been asking for two days. The dreamer Stephan Heller came to the temple of Flame three days ago at dusk, with a woman of our world, though he did not give her name."

She came to her feet. "So I was hours behind them! You—"

But Nasht interrupted, "*Listen,*" and in a more natural voice, added, "I see you are still as unrestrained as ever you were, Veline. Leaving our lands is always easy for dreamers—just wake up—but Stephan Heller wanted his companion to cross. He did have one of the silver keys that opens the Upper Gate; yet it is ordained that people of the Six Kingdoms may not pass into the waking world, so we barred their passage. That night, he prayed to the Flame, and shortly after, my fellow priest Kaman-Thah had a vision. It was an edict from an Elder One, demanding that she be allowed to pass. So we stepped aside."

Vellitt turned from her pacing. "I could have overtaken them! You've wasted *days*, Reon."

"Sit *down*, Veline. You're giving me a headache," Nasht said, sounding in that moment so like the friend of her youth that she did so, leaving unspoken all the hot words that warmed her mouth. "We didn't know she was followed, but we couldn't have refused the edict in any case.

But this afternoon, the Flame spoke to me. It was a single piece of information only, like a thunderclap in my mind: that Clarie Jurat is scion of a god."

Vellitt shook her head. "No. Her father is a burgher of Ulthar. She was born there. He owns shares in the Wool-market."

Nasht said musingly, "Actually, I should have guessed when I saw her—she has the look of the people of Leng."

"Hypothetical Leng . . ." Vellitt had grown up on stories of that icy and inhumane plateau bounded to the north by the great mountain Kadath, where the gods half-slept in blind, muttering madness beneath the malicious eyes of their divine keepers.

"*Not* hypothetical," he said. "I've been there."

"It's impossible."

He shook his head. "Some of the stories we learned as children are true. At times, a god escapes from Kadath, takes human form, and lives in Leng; and for a while he thinks a little as we do: he loves, he dreams, he drinks wine and laughs at jokes and picks fights in taverns. Clarie Jurat's grandfather escaped and fell in love with a local woman. After a year or two he returned to Kadath—"

"Leaving her alone," Vellitt said.

"Not by choice, I expect. There's no real escape from Kadath, even for the gods. Their keepers find them and drag them back and they become mad and forgetful again, though they dimly recall their lost loves, and if they can, they watch over their descendants. No: he was taken back to Kadath. But. His lady had a daughter who married an Ulthar burgher."

Vellitt took a breath. "And their daughter is Clarie Jurat."

"Their daughter is Clarie Jurat," Nasht assented. "That god was a jealous protector of his daughter until she died. It will not be different for Clarie."

"So was it her grandfather that commanded her passage?"

Nasht frowned. "No, which troubles me. It can't have been him. I know the wheres and wherefores of many gods. The Elder One that is Clarie Jurat's grandfather sleeps on his silk-draped couch on Kadath, and he has slept like that, deranged and dreaming, for many years."

Vellitt rubbed her eyes. "But why would another god care?"

"Motives and motives. Love; hate. What if Clarie Jurat's loving grandfather awakens and finds her gone out of this world? Rage, vengeance, reprisal and annihilation. I think *that* is the intention of the god that sent the vision."

"Ulthar." Of course.

The gods of the dream-realms were vicious, angry, and

small. History was filled with tales of their irrational rages and disproportionate vengeances, of cities buried in poisonous ash, of garden-lands laid waste. Annihilation. In her far-travelling days, she had walked in god-blasted wastelands. There were so many of them: a transparent plain that was a city buried in glass, the buildings intact and perfectly visible beneath her feet, but the bodies gone except for stained hollows in their shapes. An obsidian cliff a mile high where there had been farmland and fishing villages a scarce year before. Gardens turned to ash and poison, islands sunk. Once, she had found a child's gold anklet, half-melted and still encircling a small, charred bone. There had been a charm hanging from the ring: *Let no thing harm me. I am Ase Iquen.* Everywhere, signs of the gods and their intemperate, petty angers.

Ulthar's narrow streets and pretty squares, its houses and halls and temples: all blasted by god-fire and melted to slag, to glass; and its people—the students and wool merchants, the grocers and stable masters and dressmakers and every one of them—all food for carrion beasts and ghouls. The grandfather of Clarie Jurat would do it, because it is what gods did: destroy things and people. She set down her glass carefully with fingers grown nerveless.

Nasht had been silent, watching her expressions; now

he spoke. "Ulthar and more. Nir and Hatheg, and all the plains of the River Skai, even. Who knows why we were ordered to let her pass? Perhaps the Old Ones play *latrunculi,* and Clarie Jurat is a coin in their game, and Ulthar an incidental loss. Or perhaps Ulthar and the rest are just ants under the feet of fighting drunkards. Or perhaps a hate-filled god revels in destruction and pain, and causes it however he may. Veline, I've served them for twenty years, and I know little more than you."

She said with a tight laugh, "I was taught to worship them, but how can I? How can any reasonable person? Mathematics does no harm, at least."

"Worship? Is *that* what we do?" Nasht tipped his glass, watching the lamplight spangle through the wine. "We placate them, that's all."

"All right." Vellitt heard the tremble in her voice; and then, taking a breath, repeated more strongly, "All right. So. I must—*must*—go after her and bring her home. Reon, will you let me through the Upper Gate?"

Nasht said slowly, "It's forbidden, but I think I would anyway, if I had the means. I have not been able to leave Hatheg-Kla for all these years, but I remember the Skai plains—the fields. The sunlight on the wheat fields. How beautiful it all was. But only dreamers have keys, and not even all of them."

"But there are other keys?"

There were, but only five of which Nasht had certain information: Stephan Heller's, gone into the waking world. One, with a dreamer who had gone questing for the pillar-city Wenč of legend; it could not be guessed where he was, nor even whether he yet lived. Another, in the pocket of a waking-world man grown addicted to ghenty and wandering somewhere in the Six Kingdoms—unless he had pawned it for the silver. And one lost into remote Zobna, when the dreamer Adrian Fulton had been seized by shantak birds and carried screaming away.

The fifth belonged to Randolph Carter, who reigned as king in distant Ilek-Vad. Vellitt nearly dropped her glass.

"Carter?"

Nasht paused at her tone. "You know him?"

"I did," and she started laughing, surprising them both. "He is a king now? Of course, he would be. Always a man with ambition— We travelled together, after you and I parted."

Nasht tipped his head with such a quizzical expression that she added dryly, "Yes, Reon, *just* like that."

"Is that a problem?" he asked. "Love complicates everything."

She said only, "For my part, no. Ulthar's need would outweigh all the rest, anyway. But I haven't seen him for thirty years—surely it's all water long lost to the sea.

There are no other routes?"

"Undoubtedly there are, but I do not know them. I'm sure they are all of them very dangerous."

"Ilek-Vad." Vellitt tipped her head, listening to the crackling behind her ears. "That is—very far. Months. And Carter. But there's no choice, is there? I'll leave at dawn."

~

Nasht arranged for meats and breads to be prepared for her journey, sighing a little as he did so. "I wish . . . but I've gotten heavy and slow," he said, slapping his belly with a rueful laugh that was filled with the Reon Atescre that was. "I don't know how you've stayed in the same place for so long without growing mortar and moss as I have."

It was still early. There was much wine, though Vellitt had barely one glass to every three Nasht drank and he did not seem to grow drunk: perhaps in this manner he had found the means to reconcile his heart to his lot. They dined together, speaking as friends do, long-parted and soon to part again: of their lives as they were now and as they had once been, sliding without pause between memory and present preoccupations. Reon Atescre had been an impish man, light-footed and merry, and Veline Boe scarcely less so, and they had laughed often then, and now as well, as they retraced their travels together through Sarrub and Parg, Zar and Xura.

They spoke less of the subsequent years. After leaving Thalarion, Vellitt Boe had continued to far-travel and, meeting Randolph Carter some months later, journeyed with him for a time. A year or two after they had parted, she stopped her wayfaring, attended the University in Celephaïs, and accepted the Ulthar position: a sensible decision, undoubtedly the right one. But speaking with Reon, she realized suddenly that her life in Ulthar had never seemed quite real. She had not bothered to relocate from her chaotically gabled rooms on the Fellow's Stair when nicer rooms became available, because it hadn't mattered. She had pretended, and even convinced herself; but Ulthar had never been home.

Nasht's story was shorter than hers. After he and Vellitt had parted ways, he sailed to the harbor city of Lelag-Leng in the far north, ascending the plateau of frozen Leng itself. "The men of Leng were as beautiful as I'd been told." He raised his glass in a silent toast, though his face was somber. "But it was cold and always dark, and the people were suspicious of me. They don't see strangers often, except the gods who escape to walk among them, and I certainly wasn't that. But there was one house that welcomed me and fed me. They drugged

my food and tied me to a stone to be burnt alive as a sacrifice. The Elder Ones accepted me, but not as my hosts
intended, maybe. I didn't burn. When I awoke, I was lying on a slab of smoking basalt, my clothes charred to
ash, and a ukase in my head like a pounding brown noise:
*Reon Atescre is dead. Nameless go to Hatheg-Kla and be-
come Nasht.* My host's fields and flocks were just cinders
and smoke. I have been here since."

"And your family?" Vellitt said softly. Reon had always
been full of sunny stories about his brothers and sisters,
and she had gone with him once to stay with his parents
for the Turfilae festival, and they had welcomed them
with laughter and home-brewed ale: a loving home, joy-
filled.

His voice was empty. "Reon Atescre is dead. I hope
they forgot him quickly." He did not smile again that
night.

Before they separated, he led her to the library and
took from a shelf a small flat object of black enamel ornamented with silver bosses and black cabochons. He
spoke prayers over it that caused shadows to move
through his eyes, and left him looking pale and drawn behind his black beard. "There," he said finally, and handed
it to her. "If you make it to the waking world, this box will
bring you to Clarie Jurat."

"What is it like, the waking world?" she said, turning

the box over in her hands. It was surprisingly heavy, cool to the touch.

The question had been idle, but he answered, in a voice of visions: "Filled with strangeness and monsters. The sky never ends. The night has a million million stars. There are no gods." He had no recollection of his words a moment later, even when she repeated them to him; only laughed and said, "Well, you can tell me the truth of it all when you return."

"Of course," she had said. "When I return."

Back in her guest-cave after their farewells, she wrote to Gnesa of everything she had learned and of her plans to go to Ilek-Vad and ask Carter for his key, return, and charm or force her way past the keepers of the cavern of Flame to the Upper Gate. She did not see the cat all that night, but when the first light through the high window was cold lavender with approaching dawn, it returned, its whiskers spattered with the gore of some tiny beast, and groomed itself contentedly, cleaning blood and flecks of matter from its face. So it also was stronger than it had been in Ulthar, lean with muscle though still small, and when it followed her onto the white ledge and back down the stairs, she did not seek to dissuade it.

Dawn departures. How many of these had there been in those years of far-travelling? And now, again.

~

Down was as wearying as *up* had been, but more quickly traversed. She looked out on what seemed an eternal, creamy sheet of clouds and above them the tessellate shell-forms and shingling scrolls of the louring sky, but after a while she descended into the clouds and saw nothing, emerging to observe that what had been a featureless sheet of cirrus from above was, from this side, no more than a single small puff capping Hatheg-Kla's heights. Passing through the horn and ivory gates in late morning, she encountered no zoogs, but she had no wish to tempt her luck and left the forest by the most direct route. By the time she crossed its margin, the westward sun was settling into a cloud the color of dried blood. She moved out quickly onto a dry wasteland of stones and sand, scattered with patches of thorny shrub and dry grasses that scraped any exposed bare skin and raised tiny, stinging red lines.

Just before dark, she found a place of trilithons and shadowy statues of inhuman form: a ruined temple complex to some unknown god blasted by its jealous master, or razed by some divine enemy, or trampled by great beasts, time, or circumstance. She settled on a ruined pavement cradled in the corner of a crumbling shrine wall, and built a fire from the branches of a dead thorn tree. The wood was dry and resinous, burning quickly with sweet-smelling green flames. Vellitt laid out her blanket, sighing a little, for her bones ached already in expectation of the hard bed, but when she laid back, it was with relief. The temple's beds had been soft and the food excellent—the priests were not of an ascetic order—but the air seemed purer down here.

She looked up. The gibbous moon seemed very low tonight—as though, were she still the young woman who had scaled Noton, it would be no great task to swing herself up onto its shining surface—but as she watched, it began to move, rounding to full as it sailed to the east.

She thought of Randolph Carter. Not a tall man, but dark and handsome with excellent teeth: attractive in the way of all dreamers, but always with an essential, solitary coldness. In her far-travelling years, she had met five waking-world men (that she knew of), and they had all seemed to share this.

She had never met a woman from the waking world. Once she asked Carter about it.

"Women don't dream large dreams," he had said, dismissively. "It is all babies and housework. Tiny dreams."

Men said stupid things all the time, and it was perhaps no surprise that men of the waking world might do so as well, yet she was disappointed in Carter. *Her* dreams were large, of trains a mile long and ships that climbed to the stars, of learning the languages of squids and slime-molds, of crossing a chessboard the size of a city. That night and for years afterward, she had envisioned another dream land, built from the imaginings of powerful women dreamers. Perhaps it would have fewer gods, she thought as she watched the moon vanish over the horizon, leaving her in the darkness of the ninety-seven stars.

From where she lay there were several routes to Ilek-Vad, but the fastest would be to go north by north-east and meet the Oonai-Sinara caravan road, which would take her eventually to the headwaters of the Xari. She could follow the river downstream, take passage in Sinara on a dhow to the Cerenarian Sea, and there find a ship sailing east, to the twilit ocean at the foot of the glass cliffs of Ilek-Vad. Between now and then, there would be weather: this was Sextilis; but with Septiver, autumn could come, and by Octaver, there would be the start of the winter seas. And beyond all that, distance in the dream lands shifted according to laws not the wisest geographer could understand, subject to the whims of the bickering gods. In all, it would take weeks, more likely months. So much time lost—and to be lost—and not even on a certainty.

She fell asleep on her plans. She awoke once to an animal noise heard from afar, and felt the black cat's paw touching her face. The air was the deep cold of desert nights, and she had curled into a ball to preserve her warmth. She made a small opening and the cat crept beneath the blanket and pressed its chilled body to her, where it warmed quickly. She laid her hand on its fur. It smelled of killing, for it had been hunting.

～

She travelled more quickly this time. Her aches changed each day, but she was growing stronger and the tricks of the road came back to her: how to tend to her feet at the end of a long walk; how to shape a hollow for sleeping in sandy soil; how to build a protective perimeter of shifting stones and noisy shrubs. Some skills had improved with age: she was silent now in ways she never had been at twenty-five, as though her bones themselves had grown lighter. Though she had matches and the electric torch still retained some charge, she took pleasure in using flint and steel and tinder to start her nightly fires.

The caravan road was not so busy as it had been before the Five Oases had been turned to venom, but she saw occasional bands of traders on camelback, and she was passed once by a courier riding his zebra fast toward Oonai, leading two backup mounts. Wild places are emptier of large predators than any town-dweller imagines, and she saw nothing larger than an adolescent rock cat with the spots of infancy still fading from its flanks; but she heard the cough of a red-footed wamp and once, far away, the howling of a pack of the long-legged gray dogs that dwell in the deserts. The black cat of Ulthar grew still leaner and dustier. It hunted for its own food now, though it was happy to take bits of dried duck meat from her fingers when they paused in the middle of the day. It walked as much as it rode on her pack.

The desert changed, sandy soil and shrubs to a dirty white sand flecked with low, flat succulents, then red-gold rocks and waist-high sagebrush. She climbed into woodland and junipers, and eventually came to the icy headwaters of the Xari, cradled in a cirque of quartzite that glittered in the midday sun. She followed the river as it danced northward down a succession of waterfalls and rapids past the first remote homesteads. She slept for the first time in a week upon a mattress, in a hamlet that had no name—no name, for they had decided centuries before that anonymity would make it harder for Elder Ones (or tax men) to find them; except that everyone came to call them the Unnamed Village, and so their plan failed, after all. Everyone seemed to chatter endlessly: talkative innkips, voluble bakers, garrulous farmers. She had grown silent in her days in the desert.

She came to Sinara, where the Xari descended in a final sparkling cascade before settling into sedate middle age and a mannered progression down the Valley of Narthos. She booked passage on a dhow leaving in the morning. The trip to Xari-mouth would take between three and nine days—depending, the shipkip told her with a sour look as he made the Elder Sign: depending on wind and weather; depending on the ways the inconstant land might alter as they crossed it; depending on whether the attentions of the whimsical gods were drawn to the slim-hulled white boat.

It was barely midday, so she took a room in an inn and called for a bath. As she undressed, she saw a stranger, taller-seeming because she was leaner than the woman in her mirror back in Ulthar; the coppery skin of her face and arms grown darker; her black-and-silver hair tangled into the elf-locks of a mad visionary. She looked—not younger than she had in Ulthar, but wilder, more powerful: more like the Veline Boe who had travelled in her clear-eyed youth as far as Lüchen, as far as Rinar. She ruefully shook her head and bathed, and walked into Sinara's main town, to find a place that might clean the sand from her clothing and blankets, and into a shop where a woman did things to her hair until it fell in many tiny shining silver-black ropes about her face, and she looked less mad and more visionary. Also, it would be much easier to take care of, now that her quest had grown so much longer. But it was a slow process, and it was nearly dark when she emerged at last from the woman's door.

The dhow left at dawn. Because there were no other women, the shipkip had with reluctance given her a room to herself, a tiny berth behind the galley that smelled of onions and garlic—for the cook was from Asagehon. On the first day, the shipkip tried to have the black cat cast overboard. Vellitt objected and the cat vanished into some hidden recess of the dhow; but the contretemps left her friendless, so she spent her days on deck watching the Valley of Narthos unspool itself, bright and heartbreakingly beautiful.

Summer was ending, and the first gingkos flared brilliant yellow against the green of those garden lands. This was gentle country, comparatively free of great beasts, so the farms and orchards were large. The air that blew across the deck was rich with the smells of ripening fruit and grain. She had not come this way in years, but the landmarks came back to her: now a red-tiled riverside inn, now the acres of reedy backwater called Bakken, now the hillside orchards, a boatyard, a silver-walled temple, a misshapen oak tree isolated in a ploughed field and bound tightly in chains. But there were also differences: a swath of fields had been burnt to the ground and the soil scarred the dark blue that indicated divine fire; and the water downstream was for many miles stained black as tea.

The passing of days concerned her, but in the end it was a quick sail. On the morning of the fourth day, the dhow docked at Cydathria's riverside wharves. When she disembarked, the small black cat appeared as though conjured by a stage magician, and preceded her down the gangway. It was hard not to see the flick of its tail as an insolent farewell to the shipkip.

~

Vellitt Boe went immediately to the office of the harbor-master, who eyed her with contempt and tried to serve the man standing behind her first; but she had taught just such young men in her Topology lectures back at the University: it was an annoyance but no more to check his insolence and collect the information she needed. There were (he told her, his consonants as clipped as he could make them) five ships in Xari-mouth scheduled to set off in the next few days. Two were sailing to Ilek-Vad, with stops: a southern trireme without a name, and a three-masted thoti, the *Medje Löic*. Or (added the harbormaster, uninterested) she might wait. Another would come soon enough. Cydathria was always busy in the autumn as ships came for the products of the Narthos orchards.

She walked along the great jetty to where she could see the oceangoing ships, some busy at the granite wharfs and others at anchor in the Throat, awaiting their turn. It was a sunlit day with a light wind that breathed salted air into her face.

The trireme was loading, a black-hulled vessel with a single towering mast, and she recognized its type, and knew better than to take passage.

She fell in love with the *Medje Löic* the minute she identified it, out in the Throat. The unladen thoti rode high, and the perfect proportions of its rigging and hull were clear. In an earlier decade, she would have taken passage on so graceful a ship without regard to destination; she would willingly have sailed off the world's edge into the abyssal chaos if she could do so cradled among these flowing curves. Beauty, true beauty, had that power.

She tracked down the *Medje Löic*'s captain in a dock-side office, irrationally afraid that the man in line ahead of her might take the last berth or even that the captain might for some reason refuse her; but there were still berths, and her money was of course good. "The cat as well?" the captain asked, for it had followed her and was absorbed in examining the corners of the office. "We've a cat already, so yours'll have to work it out with Finellio, but *Medje*'s a big boat. We're scheduled into dock tomorrow night for loading. Stay at the Red Dog, and we'll contact you there."

The rest of the day was spent in errands. She exchanged two of the letters of credit for more gold, grateful for the Bursar's foresight, and walked up to Cydathria's High Town to purchase the things she would need for a journey that had stretched from days to months. She showed her credentials at the scholarium and was admitted to their library, where she wrote to Gnesa. She found a narrow shop she knew of old and bought a quire of paper and new pens for the voyage, and returned late to the Red Dog.

The next day, she took a ferry across Xari-mouth to Jaren, to see the home of her childhood. The town did not appear to have changed much, everything a smaller, stodgier version of Cydathria: the short granite wharfs for such boats as could brave the shallows on this side of the harbor; the warehouses, shops, and inns of Jaren-bas, crammed between the waterfront and the rosy cliff; the zigzag road and clever zebra-propelled funicular up to Jaren-haut: the smell, omnipresent, of the sea. In Jaren-haut, she walked along the High Street, past the shop where her mother had had her shoes made and the arcade where they had bought milk and vegetables and meat, though the flescher was gone, replaced by a man who sold green- and blue-veined cheeses. The confectionery was still there, and still smelled of buttercream and sugar and baking. Nothing inside had changed, not even the order in which the sweets were arranged, but she did not recognize the woman behind the counter.

She took the right turn onto Lebië, a lane too steep for wheels. It had been possible to see Jaren's wharves from the top of the maple tree at the end of Lebië, and each day, she and her brother had watched the ferries from Cydathria, to look for the tiny dark upright figure of their father. They knew to the minute how long it took for him to get to Jaren-haut, so they met him when he came off the funicular. He solemnly paid them a penny each to carry home his folio and any parcels there were.

When she had been small, Vellitt had indulged the fantasy all children had, that these were not her parents, that someday an Elder One, kindly, wise, and handsome, would reclaim her. It had not been until after her father's death that she realized the father-god of her imaginings was exactly like him.

Their mother's absences were harder to predict, for she had been a sometime sailor even after her marriage. This happened whenever she could find a ship that took women as crew, though there were few, mostly just hoppers shuttling between Cydathria and Hlanith; occasionally an oceangoing xebec. She had not returned from one of her rare blue-water trips, when her ship had been pulled underwater by something immeasurably vast and hungry. The news had come to Jaren in Vellitt's sixteenth summer. Her father made her promise never to sail, but when he died in her nineteenth year (pneumonia; it had been a terrible winter), she bought passage on the first ship to leave after the funeral, a schooner running to Sarkmouth, where the dark marshes of Lomar met the Cerenarian Sea's icy western reaches. Lomar was at all times grim, and in the month of Gamel it was also bitterly cold and windy, the air laced with acrid snow; but she responded to its bleakness as a reflection of her own sorrow. She did not come back to Jaren for five years. Her brother had in that time married a humorless woman and grown stern. He was gone now, as well.

Their house remained, a tall, slim structure still painted blue-gray, but the shutters were vermilion now instead of green, and beneath the windows, the small pine trees in urns had been replaced by pots of ceramic nightflowers. After a time, she walked back down through Jaren, returning to Cydathria just as the sun set.

There was a message awaiting her at the Red Dog: the *Medje Löic* was at the Sea-Eel Wharf, taking in cargo and supplies. Passengers were advised to report to the thoti in the morning.

～

The College had a triannual tradition of presenting a University play during Somar-term and Vellitt had occasionally assisted behind the scenes. The frenzied activity on the *Medje Löic* reminded her a little of that, the decks crammed with sailors and shore workers racing in interleaving patterns without collisions as they loaded the last cargo and stores.

She watched from the upstairs parlor of the tavern at the end of the wharf—also called the Sea-Eel—where the passengers had been sent to keep them out of the way. They clustered at the windows or sat writing final letters: mostly solitary men in the carefully inconspicuous clothing that marked experienced travellers; but also a small party of traders from Kled unafraid to mark their wealth with the excellence of their jackets; a courier and his guard in green-and-yellow livery; and a chatty man who introduced himself to everyone, even her, claiming to be from Rinar. His accent and ornate layered tunics were not quite perfect, and she pegged him for the commoner sort of shipboard grifter, surprised that the captain had not seen through him and barred passage. He must have paid well.

One of the solitary men had the look to her of a fartraveller. She knew that expression, that posture: she had seen it in herself for years and learned to recognize it in others. When he looked at her, did he see it as well? No, she was settled: Professor of Maths at Ulthar: friends, a hobby of botany, her rooms. This cat, currently curled beneath one of the chairs watching everyone's feet with an engaged, assessing air.

She was the only woman, of course, but she was used to that. In her years of far-travelling, she had met a few others like her, though they usually wayfared with a husband—legal or common-law or false—for too many men misunderstood a woman who travelled alone. Sometimes she and Reon Atescre had pretended to be married as being easier for them both. So had she and Randolph Carter, though in that case there *had* been love, she thought. As a young woman, when she had been beautiful and had worn her hair short and her clothes loose to conceal that fact, she had known all the signs of men and read them well enough that she had been successfully robbed only three times and raped once; but none of those had burned from her the hunger for empty spaces, strange cities, new oceans.

Final embarkation was in late afternoon. Her cabin was a near-perfect cube of teakwood scarce taller than she, with a built-in bunk, clipping hooks for clothing, a little folding desk, and, to her delight, a porthole, though it would not open. Vellitt unpacked quickly. Following her into the room, the cat assumed immediate possession of a yak-wool scarf she tossed for a moment upon the bunk. "I need that, cat," she warned, but it only curled tighter and gazed up with bright eyes. In the end, the scarf remained there for the rest of the voyage.

She visited the two public cabins assigned to passengers. The dining cabin's single table was not quite large enough for them all to eat together—they were thirteen—and so, she was told, people if they chose might take their meals in the main cabin, apart from the others. The Kled traders had already claimed for themselves one of the main cabin's tables, and had laid out the first arrangement of tiles for a game that she knew from experience would take days to complete. There were other tables and chairs, a selection of small stringed instruments, and a single cabinet crammed with the sorts of books people read on long voyages: lengthy biographies, mountaineering sagas, popular page-turners from twenty years back, a few classics of the sort that go unread unless there are no alternatives.

The *Medje Löic* left the wharf at dusk, picking its way to an anchorage in the Throat. Vellitt stood on deck for a time, watching the torch lights of Jaren and the gas-jet glow of Cydathria, then slept soundly in her narrow, rocking bed. She did not dream, nor did she feel the first living swell of the sea along the thoti's hull as it weighed anchor and began its voyage.

~

The *Medje Löic* was a beautiful sailor; and with the wind in a fair quarter, the air cool, and the days Septiver-bright, Vellitt spent much of her time on the aft deck, watching the land pass, or else gazing up through the layered, complex geometries of the wine-colored lateen and settee sails to the foliant sky beyond. The man she had identified as another far-traveller also preferred the aft deck, and they spoke occasionally, as when he pointed out the flying city Serranian, so far to port and so high that she could barely see the pink-marble towers against pillaring cumulus clouds. Tir Lesh Witren was his name.

This was shore-hopping, the land always in sight to starboard. They passed the jungles of Kled, league after league of rolling hills above rocky shoreline, cloaked entirely in a surprising lush green, for the trees of Kled did not lose their leaves in winter. The air was rich with spices and flowers, and she took in great lungsful. At night she saw scatterings of light ashore, as of towns lit by gaslight or even electricity.

At first, she ate in the crowded dining cabin, but the other passengers had little to say to her and she found their conversation (all of trade and card games) dull, so she began to take her meals in the main cabin, reading books she found on the crowded shelves, or content in her thoughts. She was joined sometimes by Tir Lesh Witren, or one or two of the others. The most frequent was the youngest of the Klethi traders, who eyed her with a certain awed fascination, and spoke with her as if she were eighty instead of fifty-five, asking questions about events of ancient history as though she might have been a witness: loudly, slowly, and with great courtesy.

On the fourth day, they rounded a cape and there was a single pinnacle of pure labradorite rising a hundred feet above the waves. In the Septiver midafternoon sun, it was striated purple and gray and blue, like the wing of a grackle; but her memories of other voyages overlaid the view: a stormy midmorning a year after her father's death when the stone had seemed to shine with an inner violet light; a summer afternoon when the pinnacle looked nearly lavender; a night when she had stood on the ship's deck with a man, and the pinnacle had been a spear of platinum aimed at the full moon resting overhead. But she remembered the kiss more than the rock.

On the morning of the eighth day, the thoti tided into the port of Hlanith. Passengers and cargo were to be exchanged, but the captain was eager for a fast return to the sea. "Twenty-four hours," he told Vellitt: "I'll sail with or without you."

Hlanith had much the look of Ulthar but sturdier—as indeed it had to be, a port town facing north. Contact was frequent between the towns along a pikeway through the Karthian Hills, and since becoming a professor, she had visited more than once in her Somar-term ramblings. It took no time to locate the last few oddments she needed for the voyage. She stopped for tiffin at a little tea house she remembered from years past—it would be weeks before she ate greens again. She wrote and posted yet another letter to the Dean. It felt repetitive, tedious to write—*on my way, still going; yes, indeed, another day travelling*—but it needed to be done to keep Gnesa and the College informed. More than that, it anchored her to her mission and her home; for as the miles of her journey multiplied, Ulthar was becoming remote, distant, in the past.

She was wandering toward the harbor and considering Clarie Jurat, wondering whether she was also walking along a busy street and where, when she felt herself jostled. She did not think anything, only spun on her heel and grasped the arm of the man who had touched her, and found his hand just leaving the outer pocket of her jacket, empty. He twisted away and fled: a tall man, pale as winter hay. She leaned against a wall waiting for her sudden shaking to subside. It was good to know she was still no easy prey, but it took a long time to calm her hurried heartbeat.

~

Of the passengers, only Tir Lesh Witren and the four traders from Kled remained. The five new passengers were tough-looking men: couriers, an accomptant with documents for Ilek-Vad, and a reeve representing a man with international interests. There was a harder edge to the crew, as well, for after this they would leave the comparative safety of the coast. It would be blue-water sailing until they got to the Eastlands.

Two priests came aboard as the *Medje Loïc* prepared to cast off from Hlanith, attired in layered robes of blue and black wool richly embroidered with silver thread. Their faces were concealed behind panels of silver mesh. They moved clumsily, bulkily; and water pooled beneath them on the scoured teakwood deck. Since the blue-water rituals were forbidden to landsmen, Vellitt found herself banned to her cabin. When she came on deck again, the thoti was at sea. By morning they were out of sight of land.

Distance in the dream lands was never constant, and the seas were even less stable. Randolph Carter had once made the passage from Hlanith to Celephaïs in three days—a feat that was legend—but three weeks' sailing between the two was more usual and even six weeks or more not uncommon; and the *Medje*'s destination, Ograthan, was farther than Celephaïs. And then back, if all went well and Randolph Carter gave her the key. She counted the days over in her mind, an unhappy arithmetic. Could the College conceal Clarie Jurat's absence so long? Did the University know yet; were steps being taken to suspend or close the College? Or had the mad, mindless god that was her grandfather already awakened, found her gone, and lashed out—Ulthar a dark poisoned rubble across the ground? The town was hundreds of leagues away, but sometimes she couldn't help but scan the southern horizon for fire and smoke.

Septiver turned to Octaver, and the days grew colder, until she lamented the yak-wool scarf on her bunk. Vellitt paced the decks and distracted herself with the complex topologies of the wind-filled sails, and the sky, so low that it seemed the mainmast might snag on its vague ungeometries, weighty as a tent roof pregnant with captured rain on the brink of squeezing through the canvas. There was little else to see. The *Medje Löic* sailed alone in a circle of sea twenty leagues across. Only once did they see another ship, a caravel that revealed itself as a pirate when it pursued them for an entire light-winded day in a leisurely chase that ended with darkness. Another day, there was whale spume on the horizon; and once, miles to the north, a calm gall on the water as long as the *Medje Löic*, which was (she was told) a kraken's tentacle-club floating just beneath the surface.

There were nights when the elapsing time chewed at

her, and she could not sleep. Tir Lesh Witren and the reeve who had boarded in Hlanith were often awake into the late watches, so she joined them sometimes in the main cabin, stepping into their endless games of chess, but neither of them were a match for her. And Tir Lesh made her uncomfortable. He watched her, his eyes too steady. He asked too many questions: about her past, about her destination. Had she been twenty instead of fifty-five, she might have assumed it was desire, or a mere opportunistic gauging of his chances, or even imagined, illusory love; but there were twenty-five years between them and it was impossible to suppose any of these drove him. So perhaps it was only curiosity; but she avoided him when she could, and when she could not she offered a bland, damping, slightly chilling civility she had honed across a lifetime.

Many nights she chose to walk on deck: the lowered voices of the watch at their work, the softly glowing wake. The moon was often gone, so she watched the seething sky behind the ninety-seven stars, daytime's blues re-placed with a thousand blacks: black touched with red, with brown, with a poisonous green so dark it was almost undetectable, all tumbled together in churning boils the size of planets.

When she had been younger and her eyes fresher, she had seen it better. Randolph Carter had told her once that the waking world's sky was not like this. "It's just empty," he had said. "No patterns, no changing, except clouds and the time of day."

They had been camped in Implan's bonny hills that night, three days out from Oonai along the trade route that led to Hatheg-town. They had set no fire.

She shook her head, a little impatient. "I know, you showed me that picture. But *beyond* the atmosphere. *Behind* the air."

"Nothing," he said. "After the atmosphere of Earth, you are in space, which is vacuum. Well, there *are* stars—billions, I suppose—and nebulae and gas clouds, but they exist in the infinity of space. I'm no astronomer."

"So many stars," she mused. "Do they all have gods? How do they not annihilate one another?"

"It's not the same in the real world." By *real*, he meant *Earth*.

She tried to picture it. "If the sky is infinite, why would you come here? With so many stars of your own?"

"Our world has no sweep, no scale," Carter said. "No dark poetry. We can't get to the stars, and even the moon is hundreds of thousands of miles away. There is no meaning to any of it."

"Do stars have to mean anything?" she asked, but he reached across and kissed her, and that had ended that conversation, as it had ended so many others.

She remembered Clarie Jurat's letter: *He says there are millions of stars.* She was presumably on Earth by now, with her waking-world lover. She would have seen his sky. Perhaps he had taken her to his home. Stephan Heller was a great dreamer here; surely he must be as powerful in his own place. He would have a palace, an estate of some sort. And she, with the charm of a god's granddaughter—he could hardly fail to love her utterly. He would marry her and she would become chatelaine of whatever lands were his, rich, respected, and adored. It was a pity she could not be left there.

But at other times, Vellitt thought of Clarie's father, Davell Jurat. She had met him often enough; the Trustees of Ulthar Women's College were invited to Incepts and Last-nights, holiday dinners, the College's annual report, and the alumnae Moot, and Davell took his duties seriously. He was already a widower when Vellitt first came to teach, but Senior Day Room gossip said that his wife had been truly beautiful—"a Ling'troh sculpture," Gnesa Petso had once said with a sigh, for her tastes ran to such. Some people had wondered at their marriage, for Davell was a short man with a crooked jaw and a pugged nose; but Davell's humor and glowing charm were extraordinary, even shadowed by the loss of his wife and the accumulating weight of years. Vellitt saw Davell and Clarie Jurat together at her Incept. His expression as he watched her take student robes for the first time had been a complex mixture of love, pride, and a terrible tender fear that made Vellitt look away, it was so strong. It must be ten thousand times worse for him now.

If Ulthar still stood. And then, frustrated with her circling thoughts, she would distract herself by watching the luminescent, wavering chevrons of their wake fade back to darkness, or by gazing at the mysterious glowing disks clustering in the ocean's depths.

~

The disks intrigued her, and night after night she watched them: patches of indistinct phosphorescence, roughly circular and no larger than her hand, she thought. She imagined they might be jellyfish, but when she asked a crew member, he only made the Elder Sign and spat over the railing; later, the captain came to her where she stood at the aft rail and ordered her never to speak of them again. His voice was harsher than she had ever heard it, even to his crewmembers, so she complied and thereafter kept to herself her observations of how they moved, changed size, overlapped, and absorbed one another.

There was a half-mooned night nineteen days into the blue-water passage when she saw the little glowing circles scatter as though fleeing from some unseen predator.

One grew larger and then larger still, and she realized that it was not small but had been instead very, very far away, beneath hundreds of fathoms of winter-clear water. It grew and grew, a wheeling diatom that increased in clarity and complexity until it was the size of a house, the size of a galleon, the size of a city filling the ocean beneath them from horizon to horizon. She observed details now, glowing windowless towers and five-sided structures—giant pentangular basins everywhere blazing with cold bioluminescence—the radial lines broadening until she could see countless smaller shapes streaming along them like platelets in a capillary under a microscope, or men racing in a panic along a crowded street.

It seemed certain that the *Medje Löic* would be shipwrecked, beached among whatever strange entities raced along those radial roads, but it sheared to starboard as it rose—larger and then larger still—until miles away it broke the surface with a sound like a hurricane, and wheeled up into the sky, high enough to occlude the gibbous moon; and its phosphorescence died in the air so that nothing more could be seen of the things that lived in that place.

It crashed back into the water, faster than gravity could pull. It was only then that Vellitt remembered that this diatom-city had been fleeing something. And it had not escaped; an unseen maw, immeasurably vast and hungry, had sucked it back down the way the carp had sucked the dead bird into its scarlet mouth, back on the Reffle so long ago.

It took minutes for the chaos of jumbled water to get to them, ample time for the captain and his crew to turn the thoti into the waves; and a quarter of an hour more for the bursting seas to settle at last.

It took much longer for Vellitt to stop thinking of her mother's death. Had her father imagined this?

~

Vellitt Boe awoke one day to cheers and singing and came on deck to see green shoreline far to starboard. It was the Eastlands at last, the Tanarian Hills and above them Mount Aran, green and grey, white-peaked with early-autumn snow. The *Medje Loïc* had crossed in twenty-three days with no losses. The crew celebrated with a day-long party: flutes, recorders, a cornet, fiddles, and drums; the men in their best, dancing quick-stepped hornpipes and flickering jigs. She watched and sang and drank watered grog, all barriers erased for the day. When one of the sailors, a grizzled foremast-man with waist-length braids ringing a dome of bare scalp, invited her to dance the scharplin with him, she did so—and surprised them all, for she had learned the tricky, stumbling steps in her youth when sailing to Mnar, and they came back quickly. For the last days of the voyage, the crew treated her with delighted affection, as though she were a pet one of them had brought on board and tamed to become a mascot. Perhaps she should have danced the scharplin earlier.

After that the ship was never out of sight of shore, and the leagues spun out beneath the thoti's hull steadily. Three days later, they landed at the nephrite wharves of Ograthan.

The docks of all towns are the same—wharves and warehouses, men shouting, wood and rope creaking: the smells of dead fish, creosote, and salt. On a promontory above all this stood Ograthan proper, fortified with titanic walls against the sea and what lived in it. But it had been long centuries since anything had threatened them; the city had grown well out into the green country beyond, and the thick walls had been pierced in a hundred places by tunnels, curious little hatchways, and entire windowless rooms, dug out stone by cautious stone. The wall in its immensity did not seem affected by these invasions, except that sometimes it groaned, and siftings of dust would appear in unexpected places. But someday it would fall, and Ograthan vanish beneath its stones.

The passengers dispersed for the day. Vellitt ascended a broad street, with terraces in place of stairs and shops that grew in luxury as she approached the town. She ate berries in yak's milk for breakfast, as being the thing farthest from shipboard food she could find. She had heard of the honeycombed walls of Ograthan and deciding to explore, she penetrated farther into town. The streets grew narrow and choked with trash, the houses dirtier until they vanished and were replaced by slum-like buildings fronted with grimy taverns. Hard-faced men sat on tumbled stones smoking tobacco laced with ghenty. She saw one man asprawl in the dust of an alley, his greasy head lolling against the stained stones of the giant wall. Even vile as he was, he had the sheen that meant he was a dreamer, a man of the waking world. She tried to speak with him but he only pushed her away and folded forward as though unboned, to vomit into his lap.

At one point, she saw Tir Lesh Witren duck under an archway: recognizing him by his jacket, as familiar to her as her own coat after their long passage. There was no reason he might not also be here, but for reasons she could not articulate she felt uneasy, and turned to go back the way she came. Returning to the ship, she was relieved to learn that he had in fact disembarked, his room taken by a man hastening to Ilek-Vad on the wings of bad news, hoping to arrive before his father's death.

The *Medje Loïc* left the next day, and after that to starboard there was Timnar, Exquerye, the Hills of Hap.

Every sight was new to her, for she had never come so far east. They were sailing into the twilight lands now, and the sky dimmed until the sun became an umber disk she could look at directly. The sea changed into something darker, though still clear. When she looked down into the shadowy water, she saw walls, roads, and movement. It felt as though she were coming to the rim of reality. Her restiveness grew. She nearly wept with relief when she saw the glass cliffs of Ilek-Vad.

~

Vellitt Boe and the black cat left the *Medje Loïc* with regret, on Vellitt's part at least. She took a room in a portside inn and immediately wrote to the king of Ilek-Vad, the dreamer Randolph Carter, reminding him of their long acquaintance and asking for an audience. It was an awkward letter, since they had been lovers and she had no idea what he thought of that now, so she kept it as short as she in courtesy could. She hired the innkip's daughter, a fleet-footed girl of fifteen whose restless mannerisms reminded her a bit of her own young self, to take it to the castle. It would take an hour or more for the girl to climb the steep road up the cliff, and longer still before she would receive a response (if there were one) and return. Well enough: Vellitt had other things to do.

Nothing she had with her was appropriate, so she found a dressmaker to make a gown for her audience. She took great pains over the fabric and cut, and laughed at herself as she did so, for she knew that it was not for the king of Ilek-Vad she did this, nor even to please an old lover, but for her own vanity. She had not seen him in thirty years and it had been she who left him: it would not do to look shabby, or as though she regretted anything of her life since—which had, after all, led her to her current state, Professor and Fellow at a great and ancient University.

She articulated some part of this to the dressmaker, who was (in the way of such women) incomparably wise and guessed all was not spoken. The dress would be heavy silk of a rich corvine black ("Like a professor's robes, but O! So much richer," said the dressmaker), square-necked and narrow-sleeved, with the cascading, trailing skirt preferred by Ilek-Vad's aristocracy. "Elegant, intelligent, and strong—but not too young," the dressmaker said. "I will have it tomorrow at noon, if you come back tonight for a fitting. And for the audience, your cat may have a ribbon to match. Or ... No, that would be perhaps too much. I must consider."

"It's not my cat," Vellitt said, but otherwise acceded to whatever was said. She paid the slightly shocking sum demanded of her without complaint, grateful again for the

Bursar's generosity. After that, her hair—and then there were shoes to purchase, and a scarf she might use as a shawl.

It was dinnertime before they returned to the inn, and she found a reply to her application: *Randolph Carter, ordained king and right ruler of Ilek-Vad, Narath, Thorabon, Octavia, Matië* (there was quite a long list here), *salutes Vellitt Boe, Celephaïan Doctor of Theoretics and esteemed Professor Maior at Ulthar's ancient and honorable University, and summons her to attend on the morrow, at five o'clock.*

She went early to bed. In the night the cat tapped her face with a silent paw until she pushed it away. It repeated the gesture, and a little annoyed, she sat up, awake, to hear a soft, careful snicking at her door: a lock-pick.

She slipped from her bed, reaching for the long knife beneath her pillow, but as she rose the cat cascaded to the ground with a heavy thump, and the snicking noise stopped. She crossed the room in a few strides and jerked the door open, but it was too late. There was no one visible in the short corridor.

She lit the gas-jet in her room with fingers that trembled only a little. Who was it, and why? She knew, somehow, that it was not a burglar, nor a man with rape on his mind. Was it a kidnapping? Was this to do with the gods? With her quest to retrieve Clarie Jurat? She remembered

Tir Lesh Witren, the way he had watched, and mined her for information. Perhaps he had been a spy of some sort, but for whom? He had disembarked in Ograthan; it didn't seem possible that whatever information he had managed to collect might get to Ilek-Vad faster than the *Medje Loïc* had. And what did it imply for Ulthar, if there were spies set? Or was it just some court intrigue that had everything to do with a king and his politics, and nothing to do with her?

There was no sleeping with such thoughts, but Vellitt was old and wise and experienced in far-travelling. She was able eventually to eliminate the pointless circling fears, and slept at last. But the cat remained awake until morning, lying at the foot of her bed, still as the pictures on the wall save for the occasional twitch of an ear or a whisker, or the blinking of its green eyes.

~

The dress: finished, wrapped in silver paper, and laid tenderly into a box of pale-blue cardboard; her rucksack and the valise purchased to contain the clothing she had acquired in her travels, repacked; the whole sent up the cliff road on a zebra-drawn cart driven by the innkip's daughter: and finally in early afternoon, Vellitt Boe herself ascended the crystal cliffs of Ilek-Vad beneath the strange twilit sky. The cat walked beside her.

The cliffs were wind-etched to the delicate white of hoarfrost, but wherever a crag had recently sheared off, they were clear as glass, and she could see into their crystal depths: shadows cast by the higher slopes and the road itself, striations and flaws, visible caves. She looked back at the sea whenever she paused for breath. From so far above, the ruins of a great underwater maze were visible beyond the harbor, with a single fleck of red angling across it: the *Medje Loïc,* her sails filled with the offshore wind, heading for the sunlit lands.

It was midafternoon when, winded and a little weary, she took a room at an inn in the many-turreted town near the palace. She arranged for the attendants that would walk with her, for no one navigated the steep streets of Upper Ilek-Vad without an escort carefully calibrated as to size and formality. She bathed and dressed—and there was still nearly an hour before she might present herself.

The dressmaker was as much a master of her art as any king's architect. The gown was exactly correct: severe, wise, and beautiful. Vellitt had no jewelry, but her hair shone like steel and iron, a bob of tight-twisted cords that brushed her jawline when she turned her head. She was older and her face was set into lines, though her eyes were the same as they had ever been, she thought. A matching neck-ribbon for the cat had been judged *de trop*, and the dressmaker had created instead a slim collar from a scrap of blue ribbon embroidered with silver. To Vellitt's surprise, the cat permitted it to be placed about its neck, then sat, examining itself in the room's glass.

She was going to be seen by an old lover, now a king. It was impossible to assume she would not be considered against the Veline Boe that had been. She hadn't loved Randolph Carter. He had been a man like many, so wrapped and rapt in his own story that there was no room for the world around him except as it served his own tale: the black men of Parg and Kled and Sona Nyl, the gold men of Thorabon and Ophir and Rinar; and all the women invisible everywhere, except when they brought him drinks or sold him food—all walk-on parts in the play that was Randolph Carter, or even wallpaper.

But he had loved her, or thought he did, and that had brought her, sputtering and gasping, above the surface of his self-regard. The dreamer's sheen and the power of his passion had for a time attracted her, but in the end she had not wanted a life spent treading water in his story. She still did not—and yet she regarded herself in the glass a little ruefully. To have that choice removed by time and age was painful.

"Eh," she said to the cat, who at the sound looked up at her with narrowed eyes. "Let us make our curtsey to a king."

~

The throne room of Ilek-Vad was a space a hundred meters square, fashioned of dark opal, a moonless midnight that glittered with the brilliant colors of butterflies and jungle birds. The ceiling was lost in elaborate vaults hung with lamps that cast a sharp electric-white light. The throne was as grand as the room, fashioned of a single giant golden opal and illuminated by torchières bearing blue flames that never died.

But the king did not sit there. There was a lower throne to one side, on a Drinanese carpet of great size and beauty, alongside other seats and a round table of aloeswood. Lanterns hung above this wall-less room on chains of such length that they swung slowly, like pendula. It was to this that Vellitt was led. A man in scarlet stood as she approached. She recognized him immediately, though she had forgotten that he was no taller than she.

But he—"Veline?" Randolph Carter said sounding a little shocked, and then more firmly, "Veline." She saw it suddenly: she was older and he had not predicted the ways it would change her. In the same moment it came to her that *he* had not aged externally, not by more than a year or two. He took her hands in his, and after an almost indiscernible instant's hesitation, saluted her upon her cheek. His guards and her escorts left them there; and Vellitt Boe and Randolph Carter stood alone in that soaring feather-hued space.

There was no question of formal supplications. He led her to sit beside him on the divan and poured from a bottle of pale-yellow wine from Sarrub. It tasted like sunlight and home to Vellitt, for the College's cellars were filled with Sarruvi wines. She told him of her quest, the journey thus far, and what was to come.

He looked at her in silence for a time, then said, "Four days ago, a vision came to the priests of the great shrine in Narath, with a message to be brought to me in secret. There is a god: foolish, mad, and sleeping. The daughter of his daughter has vanished from these lands, and the oracle was of the results should he awaken and find her gone—the Skai valley in fire, from Mount Lerion to Sarrub and the Karthians, and even into the zoogs' forest."

Vellitt put her head into her hands, suddenly faint.

"It was an *oracle*, not a prophecy," Randolph said. "It hasn't happened, not yet, but the vision warned that mischief-making gods are even now whispering into his ear and tickling his feet so that he shifts restlessly upon his couch. And more: the vision cautioned that there are yet other gods who do not care either way about him, but will prevent any attempt to retrieve the girl." He sighed. "So many gods, so many factions and politics and petty resentments. If you are the one seeking her, then you are the one they hunt."

She recounted the attempt to break into her room, and of Tir Lesh Witren on the ship, and added, "It did not seem to me that any of the usual reasons applied. For this, then, I suppose?"

He said with decision, "You had better stay here tonight." Summoning an attendant, he gave orders, and when the man was gone, continued with some satisfaction, "I do not think even a god's followers will seek to harm you beneath this roof."

"Thank you." Vellitt leaned forward. "You've heard my situation. Randolph, will you give me the silver key that opens the Gate? You can see how critical it is. I'll return it myself or have it brought back to you."

But Carter was already shaking his head, and his face expressed an inward grief that seemed inapt for the situation. "I don't have it. It's gone and I don't know where, whether it was stolen, or I hid it somewhere to keep it safe from theft, or—or something else. Thus far I've been able to remain, but I feel it: the real world dragging at me like gravity. There is coming a time when I'll lose this fight and fall back into the waking world. And without the key, I'll be trapped there."

He pinched the bridge of his nose, a homely gesture that brought his essential nature back to her as his unchanged face and voice had not. Thirty years ago, she would have crossed the space between them, touched the frowning line between his brows with a fingertip, and kissed him. Even now she felt the impulse ground into her muscles, but she had larger concerns.

"Then Ulthar cannot be saved?" She thought of it: Ulthar; but also Nir and Hatheg and all the little inns and farmhouses; the shepherds and the ox-drivers; Gnesa Petso and the Bursar and Derysk Oure; the toll-taker at the bridge with her practiced tale of human sacrifice; the man renting punts on the Aëdl, the Eb-Taqar Fellows with their elaborate Flittide parties; the girl in the Woolmarket who had taught her monkey to curtsey for coins—so many men and women and children. And everyone gone. She took a breath. "There *must* be alternatives."

They talked on. More wine was brought, and cakes and dates and little curls of an indescribably tender meat, which they ate absently with their fingers as they spoke. There *were* alternatives, six that Carter knew of, all so dangerous that there was evidently no need of locks and keys.

One was a cave deep in the Tanarian Hills behind Celephaïs, where the grassy hills grow dry and turn to badlands, and eventually the great Eastern desert. But that route was forbidden by ancient edicts and, while Kuranes (the king there) was Carter's once-friend and ally, he was old and would not challenge the ancient ways. If she went, she would have to enter the hills in secret.

Or, if she had money enough and did not fear treachery, she might take passage on one of the black tall-masted triremes that could sail to the moon itself. It was alleged that one might cross into the waking world by traversing its shattered regolith, but Carter did not know the details of how that might be done, nor how to descend from there to waking Earth.

The plateau of Leng under the shadow of Kadath was rumored to cross the boundaries of all worlds; but having stated that, they discarded the prospect, knowing that it was, of all options, the worst.

There was a ghenty den in distant Rinar, a few steps from the city's great market. One entered an unnamed alley and spoke certain words into a star-shaped aperture cut into a door, and if the words were the correct ones, the door would be opened. The den was so thick with the mingled smoke of tobacco, thagweed, hemp, and ghenty that it was impossible even to cross the room unaltered. If one entered any of the curtained alcoves, it was easy to judge the eerie visions contained within as hallucinations. "But they're not," said Carter to Vellitt. "The fourth opening to the left leads to the real world."

"That doesn't sound so hazardous."

"Then I have misspoken. There are things behind those curtains that would destroy you merely by being seen."

"I am not so weak," she said, angry.

"You could be made of steel and diamond, Veline, and it wouldn't matter. Some of the alcoves open onto the space between the stars. The Other Ones would find you there."

She sighed. "What else, then?"

Or, the cats might aid her. The small black cat in its blue collar had accompanied Vellitt to her audience and been well rewarded: Carter had saluted it with honor as a noble of its species, and it had been served with its own fine foods: mountain-clear water, minced mice, and a tiny fish still flipping its tail in a lapis dish. Now he stroked it where it lay upon his knee. Of course, he had always been wise in the ways of cats, valuing them above entire races, many men, and most women. "The cats have their own secret routes. They've saved me before this," he said.

"Would the cat aid me? Would you, little one?"

Carter consulted (so it *was* true that he could speak the language of cats), but after the colloquy, he shook his head. "She would willingly, but she tells me that it's not possible for men of the dream lands to travel thus. Or women," he added, perhaps remembering Veline Boe's ill-advised attempt in her youth to climb Mount Ngranek, of which it was said that no *man* could ascend and stay sane.

And so it came down to the secret paths of the ghouls. They both knew something of the creatures, who dwelt in decayed packs in the unlit under-realms. Scattered through those ichor-wet caverns and tunnels were their secret routes into the graveyards, dead-fields, and necropolises of a hundred worlds. Carter had once had friendships among them, though their support many years earlier for a quest of his had brought the deaths of many. "So do not tell them I sent you," he ended with a wry expression; "not until you know whether they associate the name of Randolph Carter with friendship or whole-scale slaughter."

~

Carter gave orders for an escort and supplies to leave at dawn. Vellitt sighed inwardly: always, dawn. She showed him the glossy black object from the library of the temple of Flame, but he could make nothing of it, saying only that it might be from his future, as time between the two worlds was not constant—obvious enough, seeing Carter's unlined hands beside her own, hard-knuckled and old, when she took back the object—and could even, perhaps, move backward. He offered her two additional gifts of great value: a password that should secure safe passage and the aid of any ghouls she encountered, and a carved red opal suspended from a fine black iron chain, which would allow her to see in the lightless under-realms.

It was not yet late, so they remained talking, moving to his private apartments high in one of Ilek-Vad's opal towers: cold rooms despite the fire that rose, smokeless and eternal, from an iron brazier broader than a man was tall. There was dinner and more wine, a red so soft that it flowed across her tongue like a recollection of autumns past. Beaujolais, he told her, brought in memory from a place in his world called France. The small black cat of Ulthar curled up beside him, purring in its sleep.

They had met in the marble streets of shining Cele-phaïs, kissed before they had spoken: Veline Boe young, clean-limbed, and radiant, and Randolph Carter with the sheen all master dreamers have. They had kissed and then spoke and then far-travelled together for nearly two years: a xebec that stopped in Sarrub, in Dylath-Leen, at the wave-swept jetties of the isles of Mtal and Dothur and Ataïl; weeks afoot exploring Thalarion and the jungles behind that demon-city; a freight barge to Sona Nyl and then Oonai and the long overland trek to Teloth and Lhosk; the pataran they had purchased and sailed alone to Thraa; the flat-beamed abari that took them up the river Ai; and finally, the disastrous crossing of the swamps of Mnar, which had ended when they fell through into the under-realms.

"Such a dark place, your world," Carter said, after a lingering silence. He lifted his glass and looked at the flames through the wine. The room in the tower of Ilek-Vad had grown quiet: the servants gone and the fire low.

"Is the waking world so different?"

"You might have found out," he said softly. There had been a night when he had invited her to return with him: no talk then of it being forbidden. She had refused, not understanding why. Now she understood that it was not the waking world she had said no to, but Carter.

"No," she said suddenly weary of it all: his self-absorption and the soul-sickness that sat so uneasily on his young face. He loved who *he* was: Randolph Carter, master dreamer, adventurer. To him, she had been landscape, an articulate crag he could ascend, a face to put to this place. When were women ever anything but footnotes to men's tales?

"You were so beautiful, Veline," he said. "Beautiful, clever, bold-hearted."

In the dim light, she could see him erasing the lines on her face, and with mingled regret and affectionate contempt she recognized his expression. He would try to kiss her—or rather, what he remembered of who she had been—in spite of the difference in their years, in spite of everything. And so she claimed a fatigue she was not feeling, and left him.

~

Randolph Carter did not accompany Vellitt Boe on her quest, and in this also he had changed, for in the youth they had shared, he would never have refused such an adventure. He stood upon the steps of the dark opaline palace of Ilek-Vad, dressed in royal robes of red couched in silver, and bearing on his head a great crown of gold, each point ornamented with an impaled silver mouse—for he was known as the Shrike to his enemies. In spite of his smooth face and unsilvered hair, he seemed old, older than she, gray and stern; and Vellitt mourned a little for the Randolph Carter she had known.

Here at last, after all these weary leagues, the small black cat of Ulthar left her: seated beside Carter, grand as a vizier in its blue collar. Vellitt knelt to stroke its head a last time, and murmured, "No ill thing, little one." It was better this way. No cat would abide such a foul place as the under-realms, and in any case it could not survive, too small not to be eaten (if some worse fate did not befall it); but she nevertheless wept, and wiped the tears away secretly against the backs of her gloves.

Carter had assigned Vellitt an escort of twenty men. Riding-zebras and yaks awaited them at the base of the cliffs; and here also was a choice gift to be offered to the ghouls, a small ebon box sealed with red wax and etched with runes.

The nearest access to the under-realms was through a cavern deep in a silver mine in the mountains behind the town of Eight Peaks, known also as Octavia. The mine had been worked for centuries, despite the strange noises that rose regularly from the deepest shaft, until the day when a rock face had collapsed and ghouls of unusual enterprise had swarmed out across the mine. Many miners had died; others had been dragged screaming away, and no one knew what had happened to them. The mine had of course been abandoned, though with some regret, for the silver had been of high quality and did not oxidize.

The journey to the mine's adit would be only a few days, depending on weather and the mutability of distance. According to an apologetic Carter, this was travelling light; still, Vellitt had a silk-batted tent to herself, instantly erected and warmed with braziers every time they stopped for more than a few moments. There was wine, and she could not help but smile a little when she was brought seasoned venison to eat, or cream whipped into a froth with honey and newfallen snow. The Carter she had known would have mocked such luxuries.

Nevertheless, it was an uncomfortable, not to say risky, journey. The mountains of Perinth were never safe, even in summer, even to those not hunted by the gods. The Octaver nights were very cold and in the mornings her feet made dark silhouettes on the rock as they melted the frost. At all hours, the party saw great shapes moving across the snowfields of distant glaciers, and heard shouts like thunder echoing and reëchoing across the cirques. The moon never once appeared, though there was no telling whether that was because it had been summoned to some god's entertainment ten thousand leagues away, or whether it had been sent away, on purpose to leave these crags in darkness.

On the third afternoon of their travel, the troop's captain stopped and established camp in a meadow beside an agate-graveled stream. They were within an hour of the adit, but it was too late in the day to find their way down through the mine to the ghouls' entrance into the under-realms, let alone to do so, exit, and get far enough away from the mine to ensure safety from whatever monstrosities might seethe forth with night.

The captain was a canny, angry man with eyes the color and hardness of jade, and she knew that had she been twenty she would have found a way to kiss his mouth, to see whether she might soften those hard eyes a little. She kept her thoughts to herself. She knew his anger was not for her personally but for his task. Leaving an old woman alone here went very much against the grain.

Even alert as the captain was, the attack when it came caught the party unawares. The doubled guards were alert through the night as they watched for mountain beasts or even ghouls from the adit. But the threat came from the heights: monstrous shantak birds floating down silently on greasy wings. Vellitt was tucked into her silken-walled tent but too restless to sleep, checking and double-checking her pack. The air outside filled suddenly with shouts and screams, the sounds of huge claws sinking into flesh and armor, and the indescribable percussion of bodies being dropped onto rock from shattering heights.

She caught up her pack and tore free of her tent just as it was smashed flat by one of the shantak birds, so close that she smelled its carrion stench and felt the repulsive flick of an oily feather against her face as she stumbled away.

She had dropped over her head the pendant fire opal that granted the ability to see in darkness. It was clear that the situation was hopeless: the captain dead in pieces a yard from her feet (but his angry jade eyes still blinking up at the sky) and the rest of the troopers dead or dying, fighting against things they could not see. There was nothing she could do, and she had a task more important than the lives of these twenty, but still she wept as she left those terrible sights and sounds, running along the narrow path the captain had pointed out to her the night before.

She estimated that she had gone nearly half the distance when the sound behind her grew suddenly louder and more ominous. The shantak birds picking over the ruined remains of the camp had discovered her absence and rose on their clashing wings to find her; it was the flapping and their shrieks to one another that she heard. With her augmented sight, she saw the foremost of them outlined as a red throbbing shape high against the seething dark sky. Silver light was just brushing the mountaintops: whatever god had ordered this attack had also summoned the moon for the hunt, and she would not be free to move in total darkness for long.

That final hour was a game of cat and mouse, but cat and mouse with a score of flying cats the size of elephants and a single mouse with wits and broken cover. She hid beneath overhangs and behind rocks, moving only when they were flying away from her or out of sight, making it to the scree field leading to the adit just as the moon cleared the nearest mountain and shone directly down into the valley. Cold white light exposed the smooth cascade of rubble; she knew she was as obvious as a lone tree as she scrambled up the slope. Detecting her at last, the shantak birds folded their wings and dove. She ran under the mine's low beam and turned to see them slam into the ground just outside. One ducked its head to reach in with its great beak, but the scree shifted, began to slide in a roaring avalanche, and it fell screaming to one side and vanished. Dust glowing white with moonlight rose and concealed the mountains and sky. Hovering shantak birds began to claw at the adit. Vellitt ran for her life.

This was the last time she saw the seething sky of the dream lands.

~

The mine's main tunnel was smooth-floored and broad, a steady smooth decline. Ilek-Vad's archives had included a crude map drawn by the only man to escape the disaster, and she followed its directions down tunnels and metal-runged ladders, past rock-falls and ancient, ruined equipment, along a seam of silver so shiningly pure that it looked as though it had already been smelted. The air grew warmer, and she discarded her coat. Except for one place where she heard water rushing at a great distance, the mine was utterly silent. She began to wonder whether the hole at the bottom of the deepest shaft had been resealed: a new worry.

But the hole was open, a ragged maw just tall enough for a single slumping ghoul. She bent down to pass through and found herself in a rough tunnel that opened into a series of caves, each larger than the one before, until she came into a cavern some hundreds of feet high and a mile or more across, and so long that she could not see to the far end.

She threaded her way through a badland stained with lichens that shone sometimes, blue or green or orange. The opalic vision gave everything a two-dimensional feel she remembered from certain late-summer afternoons in Evat, so long ago. Living creatures (or what passed for living) glowed slightly red—including the night-gaunts overhead, crisscrossing the cavern on silent batlike wings. She was still being hunted.

She paused only when fatigue left her clumsy and stumbling. The water in her canteen was lukewarm but sweet, and in its scarcity all the sweeter: not every stream would be water, and not even the water here was safe. Her pemmican would be her only food until she found ghouls, for, though she could not eat what they did, they might at least tell her which fungi or lichens were not poisonous.

Vellitt knew a little of ghouls' ways. Some lived in cities taken by guile and violence from ghasts or even gugs;

others lived in nomadic troops; and still others dwelt alone, though these last did not live long. Troops tended to rove near their exits into the worlds in which they fed; if she could find such a group that delighted in the graveyards of Earth, she might shorten her journey. In the meantime, she must avoid capture by the patrolling night gaunts—or any other beasts: there would be ghouls eager to betray her, ghasts, gugs, and yet other, unnamed monsters.

The cavern floor descended, opening out until she was in a space so big she could not imagine how the unsupported folds and heavy blocks of the roof did not collapse and bury them all: even more so when she realized that it was running with water, and that she was beneath the twilit sea she had traversed in the *Medje Loïc*. She had a flash of memory—red sails against a shifting blue sky, the smell of salt—but it seemed unreal, impossibly beautiful compared to these reeking caverns, the strange, sickening flatness of the opalic vision.

As she descended, the badlands turned to what she could only think of as woodlands, a thick forest of towering mushrooms with trunk-like stipes that dropped squirming spores the size of infant mice onto her head and arms. When the agaric forest thinned, she found herself in a maze of close-set stalagmites, where in a small clearing she saw the first sign of occupation: a seven-sided flat stone many feet across and no higher than her knee, thick with crimson lichens and tiny mushrooms like the lolling tongues of voles. She felt such a cold creeping horror in its proximity that she fell to her knees retching, and crawled, blind and sick, until she knew no more.

She awoke to the sound of feathers: an eyeless bird inches from her face, plucking one of the tight twists of her hair with its hooked beak. She flinched away with a cry, and at the sound it cupped its wings and rose silently. It was impossible to guess how much she had slept, but the retching sickness she had felt since approaching the seven-edged stone was gone. She ate and drank: food enough for five days if managed carefully, but only another two days of water. When she ran out, would she grow desperate enough to drink whatever flowed in the dark streams that crossed her path? And later: would she eat the tiny many-legged things that collected in damp places, or would she turn to larger prey?

Shouldering her pack, she walked until stalagmites gave way to another forest of tall sturdy-stiped mushrooms trailing shredded veils like willow wands. She began to forget that it had not always been like this. The cavern smelled of opened graves, of decaying fungi and carrion. The interminable sounds of moisture became a bland gray noise that faded in her ears until she heard only her own footsteps and the breath in her lungs.

She came to the abrupt end of the not-woodland and, startled, looked up from her feet across a marsh to a meadow of lichens furled like ferns into waist-high coils: everything dim but entirely crisp and depthless. Far to her left was a patch of the faintest possible blue light reflecting onto the swelling folds of the cavern's ceiling: a ghast city, for ghouls disliked the smell of the lichens that cast that light, and gugs avoided all light. To her right the cavern wall rose to the ceiling in slopes and ledges, perfect ghoul terrain. She hoped the crags were not too steep; she had been a great climber in her youth, but that had been long ago.

The marsh's surface was scummed over with a weed that seethed restlessly. She had no desire to touch that strange, writhing skin, and was contemplating her alternatives when she heard the meeping screams of a ghoul, too desperate or frightened for silence, and the splashing of bare paws racing through shallow water—and following, a low-pitched, horrid hooting. She had been carrying her machete; she limbered her wrist and stepped back into the cover of the mushroom-trees.

A young ghoul stumbled into sight, terror written in every line of its shambling form, its sloping, long-jawed features. It had been running through scummy water that came only as high as its reversed ankles; it waded deeper, until the weedlike scum swarmed against its thighs. But it would go no farther and it turned at bay. Hooting with triumph, a dozen hippocephalic ghasts burst from the trees across the marsh: sport hunters, for the long barbed spears they carried in their bifurcated forehooves were too small-tipped to kill the ghoul, and would only cripple it. There was nothing she could do, but in the end neither ghoul nor ghast escaped, for the scummy surface of the marsh rose up and swept over them all, dragging them beneath the weed in a froth of frenzied struggles. She found another way past the marsh and into the meadow beyond.

It was not so long after this that she found signs of a ghoul troop's camp tucked under an overhanging crag. Half-gnawed bones, organs left to soften with rot, and horrible souvenirs were scattered among rumpled mounds of shredded corpse-clothes and the hair of dead women: nests. Everything showed signs of recent occupation, so she called out the passwords she had been given, adding a few stumbling glibbers of her own: that she had a gift for the eldest ghoul, and a request.

One and then five, and then in the dozens and scores, the ghouls emerged from their hiding places and surrounded her. Almost, she wished that she did not have the opalic vision, for they were the stuff of darkest nightmare, somewhat human in form and yet insufficiently so:

the reversed hinges of their knees and ankles; the long, many-jointed fingers; the soiled fur that covered their sagging, quasi-human torsos. Worst were the small intelligent eyes set into their decayed canine faces. They crept near, the smallest ones approaching closely enough to touch her clothing and skin with their cold, small, rubbery paws. She set her jaw and repeated her passwords.

Eventually, the oldest of them approached, and Vellitt offered it—*her*; it was a female—the black box Carter had supplied as a gift. The eldest snatched it from Vellitt's hands and slouched away clutching it to her empty drooping dugs. When she returned a brief time later, surrounded by a vile miasma yet smacking her chops as though at a pleasant remembered flavor, she meeped that Vellitt Boe was to be accorded every ghoulish courtesy.

They offered their choicest food and drink. She refused politely, indicating that it would all be poison to her, but that clean water would not be unwelcome. Though clearly thinking a little less of her for her delicacy, they supplied this and fell to the feast they had fashioned themselves.

As they ate, Vellitt explained her quest to the waking world but did not elaborate the reasons. They would not care whether Ulthar and the Skai valley were destroyed, except as it afforded a bumper harvest of corpses; she did not want them tempted. They expressed great excitement at the undertaking, for ghouls are a fervent lot; and after much conversation, a number of the younger ones declared the intention of escorting her, as they had heard stories of waking-world graveyards and wanted to taste their dainties. The eldest sighed heavily and assigned an old female to accompany the party, for the young were always foolish and might get their honored charge killed, or even forget the sacred nature of the passwords and eat her themselves.

$\sim$

By the time they left, the party had swelled to twenty or so: the reluctant elder assigned to the task, a few middle-aged ghouls, and many youths, mostly female. Their goal was a cellar in a harbor city on the skirts of the ragged mountains that conceal Leng from the Cerenarian Sea. In that cellar was a staircase only ghouls knew, which led up through the thick-walled chimney of an ancient inn and terminated in the waking world. No ghouls of their troop had climbed those stairs for a century, and there was no telling into which waking-world graveyard they might emerge. Vellitt Boe knew little of the dimensions of the waking world: she could only hope the graveyard would not be too far from Clarie Jurat.

The party moved faster than she would have expected,

quickly ascending the cavern wall and passing through
a great natural archway to enter a chain of smaller caves
and tunnels. Each carried something—a pelvis to gnaw,
an oversized club made from the ulna of a gug's arm,
a thick-mossed gravestone—and loped tirelessly. Whenever there was water to cross, the ghouls plashed
through, holding their gravestones and bones overhead
as they paddled; and Vellitt followed, there being no
options.

There was a horrid festiveness to the young females'
enthusiasm, and a grotesque familiarity as well, for they
reminded her of nothing so much as the students of
Ulthar Women's College—Raba Hust, Derysk Oure,
Therine Angoli, and the rest. For their part, the adults
might almost have been Fellows of the College, long-
suffering and largely ignoring their charges except when
they grew too noisy. Seeing them all in this way would
for a time decrease her ongoing horror until, listening to
the younger ones meeping over some treat, she would remember that the bones they bickered over were human.
And yet, why should it matter? The dead did not need
those bones.

Ghasts and gugs were larger than ghouls but somehow
less horrible to Vellitt. At least there was no hint of hu-
manity in those monstrous forms, no glimmer of human
intelligence in their eerie eyes. With the ghouls, it was

hard not to see the possibility of her own degeneration in their forms and manner, as though the only thing between her and ghoulishness was the almost accidental hinging of her legs. Vellitt felt her jaw sometimes, to feel whether it were narrowing, elongating into something sloping and canine.

They did not rest on any schedule Vellitt could determine, and she walked sometimes in an exhausted daze. She had not known she was capable of such travelling. When they did stop, she dropped to the stony floor as though in a faint, too tired even to find a wall to sleep beside.

Once she woke to feel a rubbery paw grasping her ankle. Had she been a little more awake, she might have spoken first; she might not have swung down with her machete and felt it connect, and heard the anguished cry of a wounded ghoul as it ran howling off, leaving behind an arm severed at the elbow. She was horrified, for it had been the ghoul she called in her mind Yllyn after a second-year Practical Government student at the College, because of a similarity in the way they tipped their heads when they were thinking. For a time, Vellitt could hear the wounded ghoul following them—lacking an arm, she had grown clumsy—until two of the others returned from a private expedition carrying fresh bones and licking their lips. She was not heard again after that.

The caverns became more populated. These were ghast lands, so the wary ghouls stayed to the rough margins; ghasts usually killed ghouls, but they also captured them to add to their herds. The youngest of the females grew very concerned for Vellitt and patted continually at her hands and clothing. It was a grotesque version of the school-girl crush Vellitt had seen so many times in the College, yet she almost welcomed the attention: watched over with such an obsessive regard, she would not be taken unawares.

At the center of one of the largest of the caverns was a gargantuan shaft leading downward, a quarter of a mile across and emitting a steady, hot, sulfuric wind. They had entered high on one wall, and she could see a little distance down the shaft. A city had been carved into its walls, with broad steep ramps and square openings, and she was a little comforted, recognizing it for a gug city. Gugs were horrible—elephant-sized; oily-furred and immense-pawed creatures, their eyes staring from eye-stalks on either side of the toothed vertical gash of their mouths—but less terrible to her than anything else in these lands. A gug city might contain horrors but it held few surprises, for when she had been lost in the under-realms, she had encountered an infant gug and followed it into its city, where she had survived for a time. Neither it nor any other gug had shown her kindness, but neither had they killed her.

When the younger females saw the signs of the gug city, they clamored to hunt one, for ghouls hated gugs, and killed them whenever they had sufficient numbers. Experienced with managing the enthusiasms of the young, the elder wagged her greasy canine head: they might, certainly, and it *would* be a treat; but gugs could be had any time, after all. Did they not want to taste the delights of a waking-world graveyard? Then they must stay focused. Regretfully they agreed, though there were complaints. But they forgot soon enough, when they passed a place where some creature had fallen from a height, as they bickered over the shattered flesh they licked from the lichens with their agile tongues.

Despite their vigilance, they were ambushed—and not by gugs. The ghouls had been loping in their tireless way down a thick-lichened defile when many ghasts surged suddenly from concealed holes beyond the defile's lip. Mêlée was instant and universal. Vellitt's machete was out of reach, but she drew her long knife and fought until it was slammed from her hand by the ghasts, buffeting her with their heavy equid shoulders, grabbing with their strange split forehooves. The ghouls they did not treat so gently. She heard their screams all around, and saw the young female who had declared herself Vellitt's protector crushed beneath the feet of the largest ghast. But they did not injure Vellitt: only bumped her farther and farther from the screams of the ghouls until, in the end, she heard no more.

The ghasts did not cripple her (as was their way), nor bind her. They clubbed her with their hooves until she was half-hoisted onto the back of one of the ghasts. She tried to slide off but the other ghasts crowded close until, with a hoot from the largest of them, they departed the blood-soaked defile. They maintained a fast, swarming lope without pause and without sound. It was a little like riding a horse, if a horse's skin oozed the smells of carrion and its mane were not hair but short writhing fleshy tendrils. After a time, she fell into a miserable trance that was neither sleep nor dream, a daze that did not end until they came to their city and bore her down its broad ramps, down until the very walls seemed to seep darkness. The ghast city shared the pit with the gugs' city she had seen before; she saw the gug arches and tunnels barely a stone's throw away across the shaft and shouted, hoping that in some miraculous fashion the gug she had known as an infant might be there and remember her. But it was a ridiculous hope, and in any case the ghasts rammed her with their horrible heads, until she could do nothing but gasp for breath and struggle not to be crushed.

The ghasts stopped at last. She half-fell from her vile

mount's back, and was forced through a small opening in a wall. A stone door closed behind her, and she heard the heavy sound of a ghast settling itself against it.

~

Vellitt Boe despaired. The ghasts did not intend to maim her and add her to their herds, but that meant they had another use for her. She was sure that they had learned of her from the night-gaunts, and were holding her until she might be turned over to whatever god sought her, to be cast into the crawling abyss or to suffer some more immediate torment—that, or the ghasts would keep her in secret until they could find a way to better utilize her to their advantage, for ghasts are always aware of the main chance and respect only the highest of the Other Ones, despising the little gods that pursue their venal, foolish agendas across the upper lands.

The room was tiny, a cube scarce six feet across: nearly the size of her lovely little teak-walled cabin on the *Medje Loïc,* but too small to serve any purpose she could think of for the ghasts, who might perhaps push their heads and forequarters through the small door but no more. So: a cell. Her opalic sight showed her featureless walls, the sealed door, and two gratings carved into the living rock. As she watched, a millipede the length of her hand slipped from the upper grating, swarmed down the wall and across the floor, and disappeared into the lower one. A moment later it, or a different one, reversed the journey. In time, she realized there were many millipedes, and that this cell was part of a highway of sorts for the millipedes.

Her knife had been struck from her hand, and the ghasts had torn her pack from her. All that remained to Vellitt was whatever she had been carrying on her person: the red opal pendant; her canteen (full, for she had passed safe water a short time before the ambush, buckling it at her waist rather than returning it to the pack); a single packet of pemmican; the leather pouch of gold and coins, the remaining letters of credit, and the Bursar's little notebook; the small black-lacquered object from the waking world; matches in a waterproof case. All useless, unless she could set a fire with the matches and notebook, and somehow frighten the ghasts with it.

And so Vellitt wept. If it was not already destroyed, Ulthar would be, as soon as the Clarie Jurat's mad grandfather awakened. And Jurat herself, lost into the waking world; and the ghouls that had accompanied her these leagues, dead or enslaved; and the young female who had so foolishly fought for her—and Vellitt herself, unable to save even her own life.

She wept until her tears dropped to the ground and

the busy millipedes ran through the moisture that fell upon their path. They scuttered through her tears and scattered along their many routes, myriad feet tracing secret tracks through every corner of the ghast city, and even into the city of the gugs.

There are many gods in the dream lands: the great gods, Azathoth and hoary Nodens and the crawling chaos Nyarlathotep that is their messenger; but also many lesser gods, meek and mad, that carry in their hearts secret affections they cannot acknowledge without exposing the things they love to whatever sadistic torments the Other Ones might devise. Certain small gods had lived once on the snow-peaked slopes of Hatheg-Kla, and (though they dwelt now under the cruel eye of Nyarlathotep on cold Kadath), still they remembered their old home, and the pretty valley of the river Skai. Others, even less important, had lived in Ulthar's Temple of the Elder Gods, drinking the smoke of the sacrifices and gazing with senile affection on their city: the markets, the homes, the squares and fountains. They had watched the University with dim approval: ancient Eb-Taqar and many-halled Meianthe, New and Serran and Thane's-Colleges, Stë-Dek, and even the Women's College, humblest of the Seven.

The minor gods could not combat their masters, not directly. But they were not without resources. In a land defined by dreaming men and bickering gods, there were no sure rules, but there was also no certain randomness. Vellitt had once saved an infant gug that had fallen into a pit and been pierced by punji stakes. Already the size of a full-grown wolfhound, and already stocky, ugly, and fetid, the creature had no neonate attractiveness, but she had been alone in the under-realms and this pierced, crippled creature was the first thing that did not strike sick horror into her soul. By the faint light of lichens, she had lowered herself into the pit and levered the young gug free. Though it must have been in great pain, it did not struggle or bite her, but held still, its vertical maw agape in silent panting, expelling the reek of carrion inches from her shoulder. At last she rocked back on her heels and said aloud, "There you go;" and at the sound of her voice, the gug leapt to its six paws and bolted. Only then did she see the other gugs gathered at a distance: adult, gigantic, alien, and terrifying. They had been watching her. She was sure that, had she made different decisions, they would have destroyed her. The infant ran between their feet and was gone; a moment later, the adults followed, and she had followed them, having no better plan for her deliverance.

The busy millipedes scuttered through the secret places of the gug city and left traces wherever they walked of Vellitt Boe's tears. And a certain gug, grown to full size and dwelling a thousand leagues from the flesh-lined den of its infancy, padded upon six paws each a yard across, along steep ramps and up broad stairs and over a soaring stone archway that bridged the shaft shared by two cities; until it stalked through the alleys of the ghasts, cracking apart such structures as stood in its way, following a scent it remembered from its earliest youth. For gugs forget nothing.

The first intimation of this came to Vellitt when she heard panicked hooting outside her cell and a terrible sound, as of something fleshy crushed between great jaws. The door was smashed with a blow that threw stony shrapnel across the tiny room, and a gug's great paw reached in, patting the cell's floor and then withdrawing. Because she had nothing to lose (and in any case, to die quickly was better than to be given to whatever gods sought to stop her quest), Vellitt crawled through the opening and stood. Its head was inclined as though it looked down at her from its unfathomable eyes, and she knew suddenly what had happened and why. It was splashed to its belly with the remains of the ghast that had guarded her cell.

"Now what?" she said aloud.

She could see with her opalic vision that ghasts were clustered everywhere, just out of reach of the gug. They began a great hooting at the sound of her voice, but the gug made no sound at all: only turned and padded through the ghast city, the creatures falling back as it approached, then pooling to follow behind them. Vellitt walked beside the gug, one hand against an ancient scar upon its flank.

~

To her surprise, the gug did not leave her even after they had climbed back into the cavern, and the ghasts had relinquished their hooting pursuit. After a time, she realized it meant to stay beside her until she left the underrealms. Gugs made no sounds and did not seem to have ears; but she glibbered in the ghoulish tongue of her goal, to find the cellar in Lelag-Leng; barring that, to find another path into the waking lands. The gug gave no signs of understanding but walked off as though given an order, and she followed it.

Time blurred. They moved quickly, for the gug did not hesitate to cross open terrain, though it avoided the cyclopean cities of its kind. It neither slept nor apparently did it grow tired. It did not eat. Whenever she collapsed from fatigue, she feared the worst; but awakened each time to find herself untouched, the gug crouched like a gigantic grotesque six-pawed cat, guarding her. The ghouls had taught her things she might eat, so she peeled sheets of rank lichens from the stones and devoured them as she walked. After her canteen ran dry, she licked the walls for the water that ran down their rocky faces. She had been thin but grew gaunt, and felt ancient, inhuman, alien and unknowable. When she remembered Ulthar it was with an abstract concern, as though she had heard once of such a place, of daylight and greenery, crowds in bright colors, voices.

They came to a cavern where she saw ghasts watching a great herd of blind, shuffling animals: humans scarcely less bestial than their keepers. She begged the gug to free them, but it kept to its silent route and did not even slow. Another time, they came to a lake of dimly glowing fluid, where the gug lowered itself to its knees. She took this to mean she should climb its back, and it was thus they crossed, her face inches above the gaping vertical mouth that split its head in half.

At one point, she realized she was being followed by a small party of ghouls: not her own, for they were long gone, but strangers. She laid a trap and captured one, a cunning female of middle age with something more of intelligence in her eyes than was the rule for her kind. Vellitt asked questions, but the female refused to answer until the gug placed a forepaw upon her chest and pressed. She squealed and then the answers came, in short, wheezing, rubbery meeps: Vellitt Boe was sought by more than one of the bickering gods, each for his own reason. Some wanted to cause mischief and ending her quest guaranteed this. Others hated the Old One that was Clarie Jurat's grandfather, and sought to torment him by whatever means they might. For still others, she had herself become the goal; the gods could hate for no reason at all, and their malice had turned toward her.

The ghoul continued, though a thread of thick blood slipped from her mouth and her voice took on a wet, gobbety sound. One god, more enterprising than the rest, had offered a village of new-made fresh corpses to any dweller of the under-realms that would deliver her to him. This ghoul and her companions had determined to earn the reward.

Were there routes where she would be safe? Vellitt asked. The ghoul gurgled: she would certainly be caught when she tried to reënter the upper lands. The gug pressed harder, and the ghoul added slowly, in gasps: perhaps, from the ancient ghoulish city beneath Sarkomand. There was a way that went directly from the under-realms to the waking world without touching the dream lands.

Vellitt opened her mouth to ask more, but the gug at least was done. It leaned forward and tore the ghoul's head free of its shoulders, and blood and brains gouted across the lichened stones. Vellitt fell back, sickened, but when she looked again, there was nothing left, not so much as a scrap of bone, only blood splashed here and there, and the sounds of the gug swallowing. The first questing beetles, pallid and soft-shelled, emerged from a crevice and pressed their mouthparts against the stains: soon even those would be gone. It was as well. At least this way, Vellitt could not be tempted.

Gratitude and horror made a heavy mixture, but the gratitude outweighed the horror. The ghoulish pass-words could no longer be trusted, and the gug was in its inscrutable way the only ally she had. If she had gone to Lelag-Leng according to her earlier plan, the gods or their bitter messengers would have caught her and her quest would have ended there. There was another advan-tage that came from trapping the ghoul. It had carried a sliver of obsidian as long as her hand and sharp enough to draw blood. Vellitt slid it into the empty knife sheath be-neath her jacket and nearly wept with relief: armed again at last.

After a forever of walking, they were in a series of vast, high galleries, crafted by huge, unknowable hands or paws. The rooms were all the same, many hundreds of yards long and fifty across, jumbled with ruinous struc-tures, boulders, building stones, petrified wood—and beneath everything, icy water that had collected into fetid pools. The soaring ceilings had been carved into fantastic shapes: venous guilloché of incredible detail in one hall, irregular herati and botehs in the next, vining wormlike fretworks in a third. These were the sky, she realized suddenly: the sky interpreted by beings that had never seen its shifting patterns, but only heard them described. It was not a gug city, yet the gug knew it well enough, for in the seventh of these galleries, it turned aside into a carved passageway where gaps in the living rock had been filled with tight-laid courses of dressed stone. The passageway began to ramp upward and curved in a decreasing spiral. Occasional steps appeared, until at last Vellitt found herself ascending a great circular widdershin stair, the gug almost entirely filling the passage just behind her.

At irregular intervals, the staircase widened into circular chambers some twenty yards across and only just higher than Vellitt could reach with her upstretched hand. The gug hunkered low and crept awkwardly across these rooms. Each had seven windows spaced equally around the perimeter. Those of the lowest levels looked down into the halls of the city beneath Sarkomand, but after that she found her opalic vision could not penetrate the veil of darkness beyond the sills, and by this she surmised that they did not open onto anywhere in her own world—or perhaps, any human plane at all.

They ascended: stairs, chambers, stairs again. She lost count of the seven-windowed rooms. She turned and turned, always up and to the left, numb to anything but the sick burning of her muscles, the cartilage grinding in her knees, her heaving lungs. Drained of energy and then of volition, it became easier to lean against the outside wall and close her eyes as she ascended, only opening them when she felt the moving air in her face that presaged each chamber. She stopped looking from the windows.

Coming to the fiftieth or seventieth or hundredth chamber, she opened her eyes and felt them pierced by something harsh as a ragged blade. She fell back with a cry, bringing her hands up as a shield, and the gug muscled past her; but it was only interference between the opalic vision and a white light that was shining in all the windows, bright as the sun. She lifted the red opal from her throat, holding it tight in one hand.

They were not alone.

A figure stood before her: apparently young and very male, amber-skinned and long-faced, with winging eyebrows and fine-sculpted lips tipped into an expression that mingled disdain and amusement and the inutterable boredom of the gods. He wore pleated robes and a headdress she could not see clearly, as though it vibrated in and out of the visible spectrum. If he had been dressed in tweeds and scholar's silks, he would have looked a little like a perfected version of the young men who attended her Third-Order Saddle Shapes lectures—except for his violet eyes, which were utterly mad. She knew him for a messenger of the gods.

"You cannot stop me," she said. The gug beside her had flattened itself to fit beneath the low ceiling, but in such a way that its four massive forepaws were free to strike. Its head was lowered, eyes on their stalks slit against the searing light, but alert.

"Can I not?" the messenger said, and his voice was musical; but his laugh was a clashing sound like lightning striking a temple tower to the ground. "The walls are thin just here, between your little world and this room. But very well, perhaps I cannot. Still, you would be wise to pause a moment and listen to me."

"I am listening." She sounded churlish in her own ears, but the less she said, the less likely was it that she would make some fatal mistake.

"There is no reason to ascend and retrieve this descendant of a meaningless god. Your quest has come to nothing, Vellitt Boe. Ulthar is destroyed, Skai's plains a new wasteland. Return to your world and pick up what pieces you can of your life."

Messenger of the gods or not, Vellitt Boe was not inexperienced in the detection of lies. She shook her head and said only, "No."

His violet eyes were sorrowful, though flickering in

their depths was the eternal mockery. "You do not believe me. Take my hand and I will show you."

"No." She stepped forward, and the gug inched forward beside her. The messenger did not move, only tipped his head and looked down at her with mad eyes.

"*I* see. You cannot stop me," said Vellitt Boe. "If you could, I would be dead already, and this chamber would be a smear of black ash. And if Ulthar were truly destroyed, you would have brought me visions and shown me relics. You are just a shadow here. You have no power."

His smile contained every darkness. "Perhaps, or perhaps I merely choose not stain my hands with you. Others will. And perhaps I shall go now and destroy your Ulthar, myself."

He vanished and in the same instant the brilliant white light in the windows winked out, as well. Vellitt found herself in utter darkness, and glibbering all about her: ghoulish cries of attack. She fumbled the pendant back around her neck and her opalic vision flared, flat and dim: the circular chamber filled with foes, the gug crammed between ceiling and floor and sweeping ghouls aside with blows of its enormous arms. She pulled the obsidian blade and fought.

It would not have been enough if it had been Vellitt alone, but the gug was strong and, despite the close quarters, quick. It was clearing a path toward the upward staircase with its forepaws. She ran. A ghoul rose before her, and she struck it with the knife, which shattered into shards of black glass in her hand. She threw the broken hilt into its startled canine face and ran to the staircase. It was smaller than the others had been; there was no way the gug could follow her.

She paused and turned on the bottom step. The gug was surrounded by circling ghouls nipping in with stone blades and bone cudgels to strike wherever its back was turned. Trammeled by the low ceiling, and slipping on the viscera-slick floor, the gug could not turn easily. It grasped in one of its four arms a ghoul, but as it bent down to bite off its head, another jumped, aiming a sharpened hipbone at the base of an eye-stalk.

"No!" Vellitt cried, and leapt forward.

And the gug, perhaps hearing her voice, reared up against the stone ceiling of the seven-windowed room. The stones groaned against one another as it heaved; and then with a terrible shrieking they broke across the gug's shoulders. She had a sudden impression of plates of white marble, tumbling blocks of coarse gray stone, and rusting iron beams before searing light broke through the shattering roof and blinded her. She cried out and the gug surged forward. Something hit her in the head. Her last thought was a word that sorted itself into meaning as she passed out: *Wisconsin*.

~

Wisconsin. It was a place. It was where she was: a state in the United States, which was also where she was. It was *June,* which was Thargel—the sixth month of the calendar here. She knew the year, and why the years were numbered as they were. Shell Lake, Wisconsin. Midafternoon.

New information cascaded through her mind. Her head hurt as though it had been struck (it had, she remembered), or as though it were rearranging its pathways; and this vocabulary, these concepts, were also new. She could not get her eyes open, was not even sure she was breathing or her heart beating. There was warmth on her face, a rough, hard surface beneath her. She was lying down, she realized with a flicker of relief. Dead or alive, her body remained hers. There was a steady low growl close by that did not change in pitch or stop for breath. *Am I dreaming?* she thought, and started laughing—for that was the one thing she certainly was *not,* was dreaming—and it was this that opened her eyes.

She was lying on a broken, rough-paved lane—the word came to her, *asphalt*—that dipped through a hollow in a neglected cemetery beside a small temple—a *church,* a *Lutheran* church of brown brick and fieldstone, plain and unfussy. Concealing the sky were tall oaks and other trees, ones with pointed leaves, *maples*; and on the ground, *bluegrass* and *fescue* needing a mow, mixed with crabgrass and chickweed. Beside the lane, a mausoleum of moss-skinned marble with its lintel cracked, and a rusted iron gate gaping on its hinge.

The steady growl beside her was the gug, or what had been the gug. The words came to her for what it was now: *Buick; Riviera*—which was also a seacoast in a distant land, France. 1971, the year it was built. Almost fifty years ago. And then everything: how internal combustion engines worked and where the ignition key went and how to operate the windshield wipers; synthetic 5W-40 because Wisconsin was a winter land, R44TS sparkplugs gapped to thirty thousandths—data tumbling into place until she knew the specs as well as if she had worked on the car herself, swapping the points for digital ignition and adjusting the valve train. She understood. The waking world had no place in its schema for gugs as they were, so when the gug followed her into the little cemetery, it had been reshaped into a thing that *could* exist: a low, slope-roofed car with a jutting front end and vertical grille, and a long, tapered back window tucked between the split, slanted back bumper; everything golden-gray with dust, as though they had just come off a long gravel road.

She stood, a little shakily, aching and queasy from the—*adrenaline*—that had turned to toxins in her blood. She was wearing jeans—cotton trousers, but women wore them here—and boots, and a dark tee-shirt. She put up her hand: the red opal was still around her throat, though it no longer affected her eyesight. She was, impossibly, clean. She felt her hair's tight twists, pulled one forward, and found it was silver and black still. There might be no admission point in this world for gugs, but for older women, apparently yes. She could feel it settling about her, what this world would expect of a woman her age. She fit scarcely more naturally here than in her own land.

She leaned against the gug's hood, feeling the steady rumble of the old V-8. The long haunch of the left rear bumper had been damaged in the past and repaired with Bond-o that hadn't been painted over yet, just where the infant gug had been transfixed in the ghouls' pit-trap so long ago. How did it feel about this transformation? Did it feel despair, trapped in steel, toothless and clawless, never to taste flesh again? Or did it delight in the bright taste of gasoline, the speed of its new muscles, the ways that clever warm hands would repair its ills?

Through the windshield she saw a jacket thrown on the bench seat and knew without looking that she would find the same things she had carried in her own world:

the gift of Reon Atescre, matches, the gold and coins the Bursar had given her. This world: did she have a home, a job, a past here? Lovers and ex-lovers, a post at a university? *Harvard Yale UW Mizzou Minnesota Menomonie Baker Oxford Cambridge Sorbonne* riffled into place, like flipping through a stack of index cards. Did she have a physician—no, a *primary-care provider*; medications? No, these were all gaps. She had her gug and the things it carried; she had this knowledge of the waking world sifting into her mind; she had herself. This is how Randolph Carter said it had been for him when he first came to the dream lands. As a youth—*teenager* was the word here—he had known everything he needed, but there had been gaps.

Vellitt stretched her back (and that, at least, felt the same) and walked onto the rough grass to look at the nearest tombstones: *Voeller. Axtman. Halvorson. Johnson.* She placed her finger on *Anderson.* The moss filling the ornate *A* was dry and delicate as old paper.

She had in that first sweeping moment fully understood just how immense this waking world was. Seven billion people. How would she find Clarie Jurat in all these leagues, among all these people? Asking the question, she knew the answer. The small glossy box she had been given in Hatheg-Kla was a cell phone, lost or left behind by some dreamer in the temple of Flame. Hers, now. She leaned into the window of the car that was once a gug, and pulled it from her jacket as more details slipped into place—*password protection, GPS, maps, apps.* The screen flared into life at her touch. There were no signs of the man who had once owned it. There was a single name in the FAVORITES list: *Clarie Jurat.* She touched the name and the phone hummed in her hand. She typed the name into a search field, fingers fumbling, and a tiny map zoomed onto a blue dot labeled *Clarie Jurat 789 miles.*

This was new, too: that distance here was a certain thing, unchanging.

She got into the Buick and shifted into gear, and the gug's voice changed pitch and volume. It was all ingrained in her, the clever coordination that changed gears or slowed down, the turn signals, the vents, the cranking windows. The rough lane turned into a winding road that led beneath dappled tree-shadow through the oldest part of the cemetery and to the main gate. She pulled into the street and stopped abruptly.

In the cemetery it had been largely hidden from her by the shade trees—the sky, blue and entirely empty, blue and blue and blue, without tessellate shiftings, without the massy swells of otherness that bloomed in faint seething twists. Blue, featureless and weightless. A bird flew from a maple tree to the branches of an elm down the street. Beyond it, high overhead, she saw motes at the extremity of her vision, and then they swept down close enough to see that they were a flock of starlings, a cloud of them, changing directions as they flew, like a mist writhing, like gnats pillaring or herrings schooling. And behind them: the sky, empty, untextured, unmeaning, flat, and blue.

She stared until a pickup truck swung past, honking its horn.

~

Clarie Jurat was in Miles City, Montana. The phone offered suggestions for routes, and Vellitt Boe took the quickest of them. The land she drove through reminded her of the countryside behind Celephaïs, green with trees and bright with crops, save that the hills were gentler and there were no mountains behind them, only clouds and the hollow sky.

She passed through small towns of flat, unancient structures; houses with unornamented chimneys, wide-windowed gables, clapboard sides. The main streets were broad and faced with low buildings of brick and glass. There were larger roads lined with big boxes of concrete and steel filled with goods, and cars for sale in glittering ranks. There were signs everywhere, white, black and every color, on the highway and in the towns; street names, shop fronts, sales announcements, warnings, advertisements. No place in the dream lands was so emphatically labeled: streets and roads did not have signs, and shops had only small placards in their front windows. Even inns' signs were pictures only. Signs were promises that a thing was *here* or would be *there*, that rules would last as long as paint. Here, nothing changed at the whims of the gods or their bitter keepers.

There were no gods in this place. She could feel it in the same way she felt the vacuity of the massless sky. The air was empty except for the smells of June grass and recent rain, birds and the contrails of jets. Gravity seemed in some indefinable way less onerous, but it was not this that made things lighter: it was the absence of gods, as though she had walked her entire life under a heavy hide and cast it off at last.

The gug's engine purred westbound and came to a many-laned freeway crowded with cars of black and gray and white and the colors of the jungle birds of Kled. When she came to a town of medium size, she stopped and converted some of the gold coins to paper money. She stopped for gas. She ate chicken—which was new to her; there were no chickens in the dream lands—and drank cold tea. The gug growled steadily on, and the freeway swept her past stores, high-treed suburbs, and cluttery neighborhoods, until she came late in the afternoon to a shining city of buildings tall as crags and gleaming with crystal and steel. She passed it, and the setting sun spread its wings before her, high cirrus clouds catching fire in the sky above the tree-clustered rolling plains. The sun set and the first stars came out, Venus and Regulus, and then Beta Leonis and others: scores and then hundreds, more than she had ever imagined. She could not attend to the road, but pulled over and watched the sky bloom. Yes, millions. Billions.

Vellitt stopped for the night in a motel: no gossipy innkip or locals drinking in the taproom downstairs, and no encircling protective wall. She had no clothes but those she stood in, so she asked advice from a civil young woman in a gray trousered suit who stood behind the front desk, and was sent to a big box that was a store. Later, she slept in a room that was a rectangle, with a black-and-white photograph of a river gorge over the immense bed.

She dreamt that she stood upon a high marble terrace and looked out upon a hushed sunset city. Ulthar. It still existed. She was right that the god's messenger had lied to her. A long staircase of porphyry and jasper descended to a Gate, and beyond it, she could see the underground garden in the temple on Hatheg-Kla; but the Gate was locked. She shook her head, and shaking it, awoke. She looked out the window and the moon was full, flat, and white. It moved so slowly as to be almost imperceptible, obedient to the geometries of gravity, of physics.

Millions of stars.

In the morning the tag on the GPS map read *Clarie Jurat 467 miles*. The country had changed in the hours Vellitt had driven after dark. The trees were gone, the land flatter. Only green-gold grasses remained; rare tight folds in the plains that were waterways marked by thick bands of cottonwood trees, and every so often a cluster of buildings and signs and trees marking a freeway exit. Otherwise, the land seemed as empty as a desert, a green desert alive with wind.

She drove, and the sun drifted behind her, up, and overhead. She felt she probably had sunglasses, and it turned out she did, in the glove compartment. The gug had no air conditioning, so she drove with the windows open, and her bare arm grew hot. The air tasted of concrete and motor oil, pollen and dust and sunlight.

The country grew rough and broke into badlands, great sections of rock shredded and tipped at angles as though they had been dropped when some unknown god's blind tantrum had ended; but it was no god, only volcanism, glaciers, winds and rains and vast unmeasured, orderly eons of time. The badlands softened and became outcroppings among rolling hills of dry grasses and brush, pronghorns and cattle. She stopped for gas; stopped for bathrooms; stopped because she was thirsty, because she was hungry; stopped sometimes because she needed to stop and listen to the voiceless wind, and watch the empty sky.

Clarie Jurat 217 miles. Clarie Jurat 84 miles. Clarie Jurat 12 miles.

~

Vellitt Boe found Clarie Jurat in a shop called Common Grounds, walls of brick and dark wood wrapped around the smells of baked goods and brewed coffee. She paused in the doorway and saw her behind a long steel counter. In Ulthar, Clarie had worn skirts, dresses, her University robes, square-heeled shoes; and her hair had been a smooth, tidy braid: discreet attire, appropriate to a University woman, though her charisma had shone through. Now—how long had it been for her, here?—her black hair was a shaggy cropped tumble that fell to the nape of her neck, and there were silver hoops in her long earlobes. She wore narrow jeans with soft canvas shoes—*Vans*—a tee-shirt, and a black barista's apron, and her left arm was marked with a tattoo that wrapped her from wrist to sleeve-edge.

There was a mirror behind the coffee bar and Vellitt

saw herself for a moment reflected over Jurat's shoulder. She looked as strange to herself as Jurat did: the ropes of her hair, the black blouse opening like a crow's wings about her throat. They were both changed, in this waking world.

"Can I help—" Clarie Jurat said in her familiar, music-filled voice and looking up with a smile, fell abruptly silent. "Professor—*Boe*?"

"Jurat," Vellitt said, and with the word, she felt as though a longed-for freshet of water had been splashed in her face, for this was the end of her quest, she thought. *At last.*

"How are you here? Is—is anything wrong? My father?"

"Yes," Vellitt said baldly. "Not your father, no. But yes, there is something wrong. We have to talk."

The bell on the door jangled. "I can't right now," said Clarie Jurat, as two women walked in with a stroller, a toddler dressed in brilliant purple and green hopping beside them, shouting, *Choc! Choc!* "Come back at seven. That's an hour and a half."

Vellitt walked through Miles City: quickly done, for it was a small town but lovely, heavy with trees and grassy lawns and shade. This was the home Clarie Jurat had chosen. The schools were low brick-made things; their grounds were filled with slides, swings, climbing structures, as though children were permitted to play here. There were people everywhere, and half of them were women. The churches were silent, sleeping and godless; there was no smell of dried blood, no stains upon their calm altars.

At seven, she returned, and Clarie Jurat took Vellitt to a tiny house of blue-and-white clapboard, with a bedroom hardly larger than the bed it contained, a green-tiled bathroom, and the rest of the space a single room that was kitchen and dining room, living room and entry. Clarie talked as she poured iced black-currant tea, proud of the house, the little wooden kitchen table and matching chairs; the little laptop she had purchased the week before—"It does *everything*," she said reverently, and couldn't help laughing at herself—the thrift-store dresser on newspapers in the center of the room, which she was refinishing based on videos she had found online. There were no signs of a man's presence. She showed everything to Vellitt Boe, and Vellitt said nothing, and wept inside for Clarie Jurat.

At last Clarie said, "Shall we order a pizza? Then we don't have to go anywhere. We can eat in the kitchen. I have beer."

"Of course," Vellitt said. "I was driving and I suddenly thought *Canadian bacon,* but I don't know what it is, except as something that goes on pizza."

Clarie's smile was golden and lovely as sunrise. "Yeah, so many things I woke up knowing without ever experiencing them."

She ordered pizza and brought two beers from her refrigerator. Vellitt tasted one: bitter, thin, and fizzy. Perhaps she made a face, for Clarie said apologetically, "I know it's not as good as the ale from the Pshent, is it? Beer here is pretty bad, so far as I can tell. So, Professor. How, why?"

"You may as well call me Vellitt. Where is the man who brought you here?"

Jurat sighed a little. "Oh, Stephan. He didn't bring me *here*. He's from Missoula—that's west of here, it's all mountains and pine trees—so that's where we went, and when we split up, I came east. Four months ago, now. Wow, it seems longer."

"I'm sorry for the loss," Vellitt said, because that was a thing that should be said.

Jurat looked rueful but shrugged. "It was me. I got here, the waking world, and he was—just irrelevant. So small, compared to everything he might be. Everything I had imagined. I thought I was in love with him until I got here." She shook her head. "It's strange, how things are: people are together and then they're not, and you can't explain any of it."

Vellitt said, "It wasn't *him*, was it? That you loved. It

was this." She gestured: the room, Miles City, the waking world.

Clarie nodded. "Yeah. I mean, I work in a coffee shop. People here don't even see it; it's like this boring job for them—but every day people say hello to me; every day I meet someone new, who is round and bright and—scattery, made out of *parts,* plans and fears and love and worry and I don't even know what. I don't know how to explain it. Random and meaningful and beautiful. I know that doesn't make sense." She gave a little laugh, half defiant.

"I know," said Vellitt. "I *do* know. I arrived yesterday—in Wisconsin, so I've been driving. No one here tells people what they mean, what their world means."

Clarie picked at the bottle's label. "And there are women everywhere and people in different colors, and it's all amazing. Science. Geography. Do you know that math makes sense here? Look at this." She stretched out her tattooed arm. A number wrapped around and around her arm, beginning at her wrist and vanishing into the short sleeve of her shirt. *3.141592653589793...* "Pi," she said. "It never changes here. The rules never change, Professor. Vellitt. Here, physics is just cause and effect, and the moon orbits the Earth on a schedule. They know *years* in advance where it will be."

Vellitt waited, a skill learned in decades of tutorials

and classes. Jurat had been her best student. She would get to it.

Clarie continued, "And they have colleges everywhere, and universities, Professor. Vellitt. I can study Mathematics here. Or anything. They have sciences we've never even heard of."

Vellitt waited.

"Did you come to take me back to Ulthar?" Clarie said finally. "Because I won't go."

"I am so sorry," said Vellitt, and she told her of a small god who tossed restless and rousing on his couch; that if he awoke to find Clarie Jurat gone from his world, he would destroy Ulthar and the Skai valley.

"That's ridiculous," Clarie said. "I'm nothing there, just a third-year at University."

Vellitt pulled Clarie upright and led her to the mirror of the dresser, and looked over her shoulder at the girl, radiant, long-eyed and narrow-nosed and shiningly beautiful. "Clarie, you're not like other people. You know this, though you very properly take no advantage of the knowledge. You are the granddaughter of a god."

Clarie shook her head. "No. There are no gods."

"Not here. But there. Gods and gods and gods, and every one of them capricious, tiny, and powerful. Your grandfather is one."

"Fuck him," said Clarie Jurat; the word sat strangely in

the mouth of a College woman. "When has he ever been anything to me? Fuck them all. I will not go back."

Vellitt waited. There had been an expression that would move across Clarie's face when she was working some difficult proof in a tutorial, intent and inward; she had that look now, and Vellitt waited. All the Ulthar women, the students and scholars and Fellows: Therine Angoli and Raba Hust, Derysk Oure and Yllyn Martveit, Gnesa Petso and the Bursar; the rest of the University and her father and every other man and woman and child of Ulthar, and beyond it Nir and Hatheg-town and the glowing green plains of the river Skai.

"This is what life is, then," said Clarie into the stretching silence, anger and despair mingled in her voice. "Doing things you hate. I thought if I came here, maybe it would be different, I could be something amazing."

"Clarie—"

Three little chimes rang.

"That's the doorbell," Clarie Jurat said. "The pizza." She started to cry and could not stop for a time. In the end, it was Vellitt who went to the door and paid the man.

～

Vellitt Boe and Clarie Jurat sat long, eating pizza and

drinking the terrible beer. They did not speak much. Clarie was clearly full of dark thoughts—and Vellitt as well, hating herself for her quest.

But Clarie put down her beer and said, finally, with a small, twisted smile, "I'll do it. Of course. I should have said that earlier, right? That's what Ulthar Women's College women do, isn't it? The right thing. Except that I don't know how to go back."

Vellitt said, slowly, "It's not so hard from this side. You sleep. I think your grandfather's blood will call you home."

"And you'll be with me." It was half a question.

Vellitt stood and crossed to the window, looked out on the sunset sky, her gug parked on the street behind Clarie's rusty Toyota. "I cannot."

Clarie's voice behind her trembled: surprise, anger. "*What?* Why should I return if you will not?"

"Not 'will not.' Cannot. I've known since Hatheg-Kla. I hoped it wouldn't be true, but as I climbed into this world—it's clear now; I've become an object for the gods, searching for you. They'll destroy Ulthar for *my* sake, hating *me.*" She turned to face Clarie. "I could go back and be killed, and I'd do it if that ended it. But I think it's more likely that I would be spared for a time—so that I could watch Ulthar razed, burning. A glassy plain."

"The gods would do that?"

"You know they would, Jurat. Think of Irem. Think of Sarnath. Like the children's rhyme—*Sarnath, Sarkomand, Khem, and Toldees.* This is what the gods *do,* is destroy." Vellitt turned back to watch the shadows pool. "I lived there for so many years, Jurat, and never thought of it as home. It was just an endpoint to my journeys—I could not keep travelling, so I stopped and it happened to be Ulthar. And now that I can't go back, I realize it became home, anyway." Vellitt exhaled something that might have been a laugh.

There was a silence.

"No," Clarie said, after eternity. Her voice was changed: strong as steel. She walked to the window to stand beside Vellitt and together they looked out: Miles City and the long shadows, the cars. "It's not his blood that calls me home—not in the way you mean. If I am a god's granddaughter, then I am a god, right? So *I* can save Ulthar. Some people change the world. And some people change the people who change the world, and that's you." She turned, and all the attention of this altered Clarie Jurat focused on Vellitt Boe, and she fought the impulse to faint from the stress of that regard.

Clarie went on, "I've seen a world without gods, and it's better. You: stay, and I will return and fix our world. There have to be ways to counter them. To fight them. I am one of them. I can do it." She laughed and for a moment it seemed as though the little house was filled with thunder and the earth beneath them shuddered.

Vellitt stumbled backward. Clarie pivoted to look at her; her eyes reflecting the kitchen lights seemed filled with flame. "Do you doubt me?"

"No," Vellitt said. "No."

~

They fell asleep at last, Clarie Jurat in her little bedroom and Vellitt Boe on the sofa, wrapped in a crocheted afghan Clarie had found in a thrift store. Vellitt found herself on a marble terrace, but the terrace looked out on nothing but darkness and the clustered urns were filled with black roses that smelled of dust; and she knew how to read these signs. Clarie Jurat was beside her: brilliant, strong-willed, beautiful, with long fierce eyes and her hair a glowing crown. They descended together the seventy steps to the Gate—and just visible beyond was a cavern like a secret garden, with fungi like willow trees, and mosses like grasses; and on the tessellated path was a man with violet robes and a heavy spade-shaped black beard: Reon Atescre who was now Nasht.

The gate was secured with a lock, shining like gold. They had no key, but Clarie said in a god's voice, "I will enter," and the Gate burst open. "Live without gods," she said to Vellitt, and stepped onto the silver pavement.

"Wait—" said Vellitt, remembering a thing suddenly. She felt in her pocket for the Bursar's little lined notebook, filled with expenditures. "Take this back to the College when you can." She extended her hand through the opened Gate and felt the dream lands buzzing at her skin. Clarie took it before turning back to Reon, who had fallen to his knees before her.

"Do not kneel," said Clarie Jurat in a voice like thunder, like earths breaking and stars forming. "No more gods."

～

And Vellitt Boe awoke, shoutingly awake on the couch in what had been Clarie's house, and she was alone.

She stood, feeling an ache in her lower back, too old to sleep on couches. A beer bottle on the unfinished dresser had left a white ring; at some point in their sleep, the mirror had broken into shards that lay scattered across the floor. She glimpsed movement in one, but it was only her reflection as she stretched and looked about.

Clarie Jurat was gone and already the rooms seemed as though they had been emptied of life, embedded in the impenetrable amber of the past. Would there be unanswered texts, an unfilled shift at the coffee shop in Main Street, a missing-persons report, and her Toyota rusting until it was towed; or would the waking world reseal itself over the place that had been Clarie Jurat, and leave no signs she had ever been there?

She walked outside. Birds sang in the shrubs beside the door, and flared up and across the street as she walked down the steps. The sharp smell of gasoline came crisp from the neighbor's driveway, where he filled his lawnmower's tank from a red poly gas can, and he nodded a greeting. Light glowed from street and tree and lawn and house, and over everything shone the brightening sky, godless and unfigured. The Buick slept beneath the oak tree by the street, lean-haunched and gray and beautiful to her; and on the hood, as precisely as a statue, sat the small black cat, her tail curled about her feet. When she saw Vellitt, she made a sound and stood in a complicated fluid movement that was back-arch and leg-stretch and tail-twist and head-butt into Vellitt's cupped hand.

"You're staying?" she asked aloud. The cat meowed again.

Infinities away, Clarie Jurat walked down the seven hundred steps into the dream lands to change her world. And Vellitt Boe picked up the cat and sat on the Buick's hood and said, "Well, this is us, then. Now what?"

Acknowledgments

Thank you, as always and ever, to Elizabeth Bourne, Chris McKitterick, and Barbara J. Webb; and to Jonathan Strahan and John Myers Myers's *Silverlock,* for the incitement. And I must of course acknowledge Lovecraft's *The Dream-Quest of Unknown Kadath.* I first read it at ten, thrilled and terrified, and uncomfortable with the racism but not yet aware that the total absence of women was also problematic. This story is my adult self returning to a thing I loved as a child and seeing whether I could make adult sense of it.

About the Author

KIJ JOHNSON's short fiction has won the Hugo, Nebula, World Fantasy, and Sturgeon Awards, among others. In the past, she has worked in editorial and project-management capacities for Tor Books, Wizards of the Coast/TSR, Dark Horse Comics, and Microsoft. Currently, she is an assistant professor of creative writing at the University of Kansas and associate director for the Gunn Center for the Study of Science Fiction.

TOR·COM

Science fiction. Fantasy. The universe.

And related subjects.

*

More than just a publisher's website, *Tor.com*
is a venue for **original fiction, comics,** and
discussion of the entire field of SF and fantasy,
in all media and from all sources. Visit our site
today—and join the conversation yourself.